William Entriken Baily

Dramatic Poems

William Entriken Baily

Dramatic Poems

ISBN/EAN: 9783337335076

Printed in Europe, USA, Canada, Australia, Japan

Cover: Foto ©Andreas Hilbeck / pixelio.de

More available books at **www.hansebooks.com**

DRAMATIC POEMS.

BY

WILLIAM ENTRIKEN BAILY.

.... Shall I call
Antiquity from the old schools of Greece?
—MILTON.

PHILADELPHIA:

PRINTED FOR THE AUTHOR.

1894.

DRAMATIC POEMS.

CONTENTS.

DRAMATIC POEMS.

THE SACRIFICE OF IPHIGENIA.

THE PERSONS.

AGAMEMNON, *the Grecian commander.*
ACHILLES, *a Grecian leader.*
CLYTEMNESTRA, *wife to Agamemnon.*
IPHIGENIA, *daughter to Agamemnon.*

SCENE I.—At Aulis.

IPHIGENIA *alone.*

Iph.   Ah, woe is me! alone to die!—foredoomed
To heir this ill so soon! What visions haunt,
As if from realms below, my memory!
I would not have the naked truth reveal
The providence of Fate; a pause must give
To fancy yet its spell, relieving it
Of the dim things oppressive to control.
'T is maidenhood would live, life's spring, life's hues
To have, as has the blossom's beauty hued
To germinate in fruit. Thus sad it is
(For flesh is e'er suppliant for its own)
To sue for being's self from him who gave—
Who is a part of me, and I of him;—

(7)

The final vital link of child with sire
To separate, to be a ghost in night
Perpetual veiled! . . . Still moments mutable
Their feelings form, impressing with a thrill,
This instant sent. Despair gives birth to hope,
And hope to peace, as perished voices come
Assuring all is well. Endurance then
Must its requital have. A father's words
Withal the heart condones, as bows the head
In bitter duty borne to sacrifice,
The gods contriving and attesting it!

Enter CLYTEMNESTRA.

Clyt. What lot for thee, my child! Deliberate
I cannot on it with what patience teaches.
My husband!—so to wander from himself
As false to be to thee; thy father once,
Destroyer now—the Hours that beat down men
To dust, their rulings to anticipate;
And thou so young, so fair! . . . Must he his own,
My own, repudiate, nor leave me plead
For it? What righteousness is there? Oh, plight
Of woman, why bid go to man for joy,
And going so, too often find there woe?
Iph. Behooves thee not complaining of our lord,
Thy husband, when as agent he submits
To grim necessity. Forthwith he parts
With me, 't is from his flesh, as much as if
With his right arm, subjecting the intent

Obedient to Diana's wish. In heaven she,
On earth we—how attain can we as shades
Regions Elysian, to espouse ourselves
To happiness, supernal there, opposed
As mortals to the laws bestowing it?
We forfeit favors by disloyalty
Unto the powers above surmounting kings.

Clyt. Alas! my child, as this to hear thee utter!
To bear a victim for the altar who,
In blindness to her ties, o'errules now me!
Sad fruit of cares, ungrateful daughter thou! . . .
Affection now grow cold! Consoling e'er
Again, welcome not its life-flame to meet
Love with contrary qualities! . . . What, both—
A husband and a daughter—turned against
The mother and the wife in one! But, no!—
It must not be confronted thus. Come, strength,
A barrier to the heart's infirmity,
To aid the mind to act 'gainst present ills! . . .
Iphigenia, we must move to thwart
Thy father's purpose. Thou, in lethargy,
Art conscious not of will. Let it arouse;
Be leader hence with mine; be rational
To risk what must be met; thus meeting it,
In reason's triumph thy salvation find.
Thus men proceed to ends, why women not?

Iph. Mother, beware! I shall not follow thee.
Be ruled by confidence that what's to come,
Though evil, good promotes. I've shed some tears;
I've pleadings made impelled by selfishness;

I 've wrestled with a spirit grieved within,
Uncertain, though achieving what I would,
To call it victory. Then heedful be,
Dear mother; for persuasion thine so warm
Falls on cold ears.
    Clyt.   Thee Aulis hath confused;
Thou shouldst be home in Argos. Loss is here!—
Salvation thine I need, in pang my want.
    Iph. Wanting supplies the pang, and not the need.
    Clyt. A mother seeks her offspring's charity!
    Iph. This same is due from thee to him, my sire.
    Clyt. I would have thee his wish obey at first,
And disobey anon. Subjected thus,
My bosom bears a share of fickleness.
What is within is comprehended not;
What is without no less is dark, not plain.
Darkness, it seems to me, is evil's own,
Not tenable by virtue, that pursues
The free and wholesome light. Hence when 't is bid
For thee to die, I fear 't is but the craft
Of men so ord'ring to accomplish what
They suffer not to be proclaimed; or, next,
Conceive I 't is the working of the gods
Upon these men, in some undeemed behalf
Of justice, 'gainst its foes to counteract.
Thus is my mind swayed to and fro—thus why
I would have thee his wish obey at first,
And disobey anon.

Exit IPHIGENIA.

She 's gone! She heard,
But pond'ring lost the sense of what I spoke.
To be confuted thus 't is pitiful!

SCENE II.

AGAMEMNON *alone.*

Aga. Unfortunate my portion if to strive
Do not I to unlink what holds us here,
Aulis! Ambition deals with us with cold
Reserve of mastership that lacketh trust
In us, and to another nature than
Our own makes us appear akin. It seems
The heart is severed from the mind; it is
Apart, with pity faint, asleep to thought,
Save that which stirs solicitude. Thus moved,
It is compunction first; assurance next,
That headlong would be first, and to prevail,
Points that endurance is a chain now gross
To wear. What privilege hath freedom's wing!
But Aulis rules with bitter jealousy,
Her winds not fav'ring Greece. It seems that Troy,
By her protected, Heaven protects it, too,
Instilling by degrees a daunted sense,
That numbs—ambition's bane!—that men the chief
Yield to—a superstition in the breast,
Which shows despite itself we objects are
Of vague decrees from high; yet so direct
Their causes hidden to fulfill! . . . Calchas,

Approaching Menelaus, Ulysses, I,
Was made to utter what, with touch prolonged,
Makes shudders steal. Industrious as I am
With reveries, unfolding thought o'er thought,
Deep in futurity to know the fates,
What pain to learn Diana wroth demands
A victim from my family—from me,
The king of kings, of those as great as I
The cynosure! It to complain was just
(Although Ulysses proved it otherwise,
Making respected and respecting pleas
Answer persuasion well) unto the gods
That she, my daughter, Iphigenia
(Betrothed to the resistless Achilles),
Must bend in sacrifice! Fruitless complaint
Is witness proving fault in making it.
Hereby comforted, pacing to and fro,
Atoning with reflections for the ear
Of Heaven, I observe abroad, and hark
As if kind Heaven is responsive thus:
'T is for thy own avail these ships go far!
Then musing know the goddess to appease
Is to have means to reach the Asian shore,
That step of glory fraught with Trojan doom.
Next conscience dictates what I do, virtues
Inspiring it; else would I feel not part
In right supported not in part by them.
Thus are the deeds of greatness born in what
Seems crime, the merit leaving to outlast
The blemish, and to hallow it for aye.

Enter CLYTEMNESTRA.

Clyt. Must your own daughter on the altar die?
To be the bride of Achilles; now not:
Felicity to persecution joined!
Aga. She's pledged by me, with honor absolute.
Clyt. With honor absolute! What term is this?
This Helen, lo! is she to be the bane
Of Greece so far, and still besides unknown?
Must war for her impress you so against
Your blood transmitted to the one that woke
Your love with baby energy, your beard
With her wee palms outstretching to displace
And pluck? Now this gift from the gods, as 't was
Your wont to say, disowned must be, in view
To gratify fulfilled the promise made
Of Asia's government to that of Greece,
You sovereign. An oracle speaks what
He wills, with outer show of truth to win
His cause, and inner error moving him,
And he, deceiving, self deceives. Thus from
A spring impure, so acrid to the taste, your mind
Contaminate proceeds to act! . . . Defend,
Ye skies, from what inhuman is!—from what
No mercy can approve—restoring us
Domestic bliss lost in opprobrium!
Aga. O wife! far Troy in dark renown must fall.
She breeds catastrophe, affecting men
With passion, tyranny and perfidy.
It is a vital force, not conquered soon

Is conqueror, debasing to endure:
Not wisdom's choice its menace to connive;
Not valor's to decline when it confronts;
But both, in concord acting, aim to serve
Through war's turmoils to found posthumous rights,
Their foe barbarous forcing to constraint.

Clyt. Doth love of equity you urge to bear
This manner changed? Is the excuse for it
Not hued by falsehood, that ashamed is placed
Behind what is ostensible to those
Who see amiss? Your nature you condemns
E'en to benignity, to palliate
So ready. Time must show it mockery,
Leading you forward to contrition's vale.
What pride is yours to serve in majesty
Of sacrifice, impressing twenty kings,
Greece, too, as lord of all, in spurning ties
Of duty as the father of your child!

Aga. Helpmeet, why futile chide? 'T is Destiny
Commands; submitting thus incline thyself.
A king's own joy is not his diadem.
What I possess I owe to Jupiter;
To him all must be first, myself be last.
He rules, inscrutable, appearing just
To faith resigned to power supreme. What can
I less than yield unto the course of things,
He forming them; by means to strive as man
Approval his to win, and thence endowed
(For such we are at best with spell divine),
In life, in death, be part of him my soul?

So innate this impulse, it would expand;
Ascends it oft, as oft descends in grief;
It as the mariner on ocean views
An infinite comprising space in vain;
Its sole temptation is the fruit of Time
(Outvying far the clustered gems of Bacchus!)
With bays by, reached to be through jeopardy;
Its standard, heroic Hercules—man's
Thought eminent, woman's misconception.

    Clyt. An Argonaut, with tale score-told of past
Exploits, your aim!—still foe to the idea
Iphigenia should be your primal care!
Is this something, this soul-search for a goal
(Which you allures, astray you leaving oft),
Absorbing passion, void of love domestic?—
Your daughter fit for Lethe's dark embrace,
By martial drift cast there! What purpose next
May lead you on I know not; but a fear
Presages that my fate, at your behest,
In turn may yield in shameful union joined
With hers. Ah, there must surely lurk within
You a perversion that, unseen of any,
Strides on, relentless, acting that unfeigned
With furtive brow, conspiring more and more
Unto a haughty soul to minister,
Your family to doom to perdition!

    Aga. So extravagant 'gainst the circumstance
Investing us at Aulis here; of Heaven
Defiant, too! Necessity requires
A deed of dread; alone, how dark! but placed

Beside that which conjoins the country's weal
To armed hosts here (to whom infallible
Was promised much), it darkness seems exchanged
For dawn. Iphigenia, so tractable,
So modest, self-adaptful to events,
So like a child in tempered womanhood,
The mandate harsh full knows recoils my heart,
Too fond at times, to bid that done which left
Undone shall peril all. Myself would fall
Upon embattled fields, subserving Greece,
Feeling the death would be a monument
Outlasting what I am. I would have her,
My child, to die, no less to reap effect
From such a cause—a daughter vain in war,
Still aiding it, her honor, too, by one
Day's death submissive to Diana's hest.

    Clyt. Husband, it looks as if this madness were;
Or else an attitude of humor yoked
With those who would undo, to raise themselves,
Your household kindred. . . . It is Calchas' sin!
His artifice advantage counts for self.
Thus comes he 'tween a father and a child.
What prophet knows the path that Time pursues?
Yet master now, assuming that he does,
He Greece instructs, its armies here, their chiefs;
Ignoring royalty, bids kings obey,
As Menelaus, Ulysses and their friends
Support him in his tragic offices.
Thus are you hedged, exaction's prisoner,
E'en to avow it to yourself too weak!

Aga. O wife! thy fears, while showing love, deny
What reason would to all corroborate:
Hence is it vain to make thy passion see;
Anothe⌐ time submission govern let,
As 't is in daughter thine exemplified.

Clyt. When kissing Iphigenia thrice good-by,
As you were leaving for the war, from Troy
You promised her the spoils of jewels choice,
Rare pearls, and weavings inestimable.
To come to this! What child hereafter knows
Its father? . . . Menelaus asks sacrifice;
Would he had he a daughter forming it?

Exit AGAMEMNON.

Alas! he, too, moves coldly from my side
As Iphigenia. Alienated,
Despite myself, I am from those held dear,
That wander spectre-like from off my path.
What can it mean? Perhaps my words to tact
Were recreant; reacting hence, his mind
Turns off resolved, in opposition fixed.
Reproof, more mild, sagacious e'er, for me
Wins not with truth enclosed within a bur,
That pricks, arouses, then presents the nut
To gratify the eye. Thus do I lose
By pleas—by labor often false with voice
Of anger, not with that of judgment true.
Oh, let hereafter be my bosom hard
The better to control its purposes!

2 - B

Contemning it as now unworthy, weak,
Be parent not by half, but father all,
To rule inflexible and masculine.

SCENE III.

ACHILLES *and* CLYTEMNESTRA.

Achil. Iphigenia here! Why is it thus?
Delayed at Aulis, waiting for the wind
To puff our sails, our hosts excitable,
Eager for Troy (in daily menaces
Her name oft heard), as martial blasts abound,
We are filled up with enterprising thoughts;
Now love comes in contrasting such the more.
   Clyt. How cold is this! Not nature's lover you.
Love is memorial keeping much in mind.
Why ask you so, nor leap in joy her here?
   Achil. Fear sees prudently, love impelling it.
Why did she leave paternal Argive soil?
   Clyt. She left it at the bidding of my lord.
So underhand!—hath he not told you she
Has come, her lover you, with right to know?
   Achil. Not he, I swear. He is obliged to me,
To whom imperial favors have I borne.
Now he from me himself aloof retires:
Is this a meed for loyalty? Yet he,
Now wisely silent, may have cause. Besides,
Within the camps are casualties, murmurs
Increasing o'er and o'er. Her advent here
Does surely not in part occasion them?

Clyt. I know not. There is foiling mystery
Afoot behind impatience everywhere,
That keeps surmises busy in the mouths,
As movements ripen in their character.
My husband is unquiet, meeting me
At Aulis here (and thus, too, after me
In haste to bring) with glances scornful, wild,
As if intruding I am thwarting too.

Achil. Was his purport, in calling you both here,
Touching not me, but other chieftains by?

Clyt. This you may learn anon. Led on we were
With aught to make us curious, knowing he
Thus caught most easily we women are.
Now here, entrapped as birds in nets by him,
We face the hazard of conditions hard,
With worse in store, perhaps, in the unknown.

Achil. Iphigenia, would he do her harm?—
No!—not so bold as that. His daughter's face
Would stand precluding even thought of it.

Clyt. Alack! I know the motion of his thoughts,
And how they sway: embodied in shame's action
His own unsettled self create would not.
However, he 's environed late by those
Who know he 's king by half, the other lamb.

Achil. 'T is hard to understand what inner cause
Now underlies with peril, proof so scant.

Clyt. Believe there 's peril near. The proof is in
Much seen, much heard. Suspicion's hungry look
Beholds. Oh, overthrow!—strike at the root
Ere the obnoxious fruit finds birth in blossom.

Achil. Aye! aye!—my happiness on it depends.
Nature is stirred within to supplement
What it owes to itself to be content.
This never is (speak heart!) when she 's in bonds:
The boundary of her liberty curtailed,
A martyr to emotion's circumstance.
Clyt. Rather say you, to Iphigenia pledged:
Discontent, having ferret's sight, must seek
Causes in secrecy surrounding her.
Achil. What must we crawl into forbidden paths?
Clyt. 'T is well to verify to self the need.
Achil. What man than Agamemnon dost thou fear?
Clyt. I think that Calchas has a motive hid,
And matches mischief with a hand, in what
It does concealing what it wants. He feigns,
And piously, 't is given him dark rights.
Achil. But Agamemnon, keen observing men,
In this deluded could not surely be.
Clyt. What scruples he to borrow, not to pay—
To profit by a promise e'er unkept?
Now militant, his very breath comes forth
As neighing courser's. Thus him Calchas finds,
And he, abetting, makes my husband prone
To countenance conclusions plausible
Each fears to say to us in confidence,
Lest power of ours confronting him defeats.
Ask you: Why is Iphigenia here?
Why are you sought to be deceived in this?
Why shuns my husband, morbid in his tent,
The broad day's eye, as if alarmed at light?

These answer all as best you can, and lo!
There follows naught assuaging to belief.
   Achil. What is this Calchas? Is he not high-priest
Of these times chosen, trusted, faithful, mild
And zealous, stored with lore and laws, sincere
And frank to strangers needing his advice?
As sinister, conjecture knows him not.
Yet with him late too oft Ulysses goes.
The Ithacan is poor; is double-mouthed,
Revolving words to justify his acts;
His love adventure and its readiness;
His knack lies in the careless use of self
To mount and rule. He may in Calchas see
An advocate, and leading him amiss
Steals to a goal productive to his claim.
The chiefs contentious nurse disturbing schemes;
'T is not alone they war for Menelaus;
Ambition's weeds impair the planter's skill;
Nor wonder Agamemnon is distressed.
   Clyt. If so, could he receive his wife, his brows
Close knit, pompous, repelling, wordy, vague?
He knows what obstacles intimidate.
There 's matter that concerns his household which,
To you and me, is fatal to repose.
With him according Iphigenia stands,
Voicing for him what argument forbids.
   Achil. Alack, against us two? If so, 't is one
That errs obedient to a stronger one,
And erring will resume anon a course
Of rectitude, her genial attribute.

Clyt. She errs, indeed! Yet she 's variable,
As if to strive 'gainst agony; then would
Betime it chide, it smiling down. Her eyes
Are shaded with dismay, or radiant
And affable; her voice hath winter's blare,
Or summer's calm inducing friends to seek
Her face to face—all in an hour. Still know,
There is intent behind the seen unseen,
Drawing these men, about whom we surmise,
Eluding serpent-like, through artifice
And labyrinth of watchful policy
For chance success to favor them. They know
To you in love is Iphigenia wed;
Her mother doth in this co-operate;
Formidable, emphatic, Achilles;
Therefore they circumspect must be. Arouse!
Treat them as holding you, their gratitude
To you as debt likewise despised, until
They prove by candor errors bias you.
If not, consider there is risk at stake,
That must be bravely met by means protective.
    Achil. Yes, yes! methinks of recent subterfuges
Of Agamemnon, which, convincing half,
Have that about them which keeps memory.
Rise they twofold in bulk, evoking what
Makes seem indices to conspiracy.
    Clyt. With me just so—conspiracy the word!
We were requested ones to interview
For reasons that the present findeth not;
We were told much that once examined left

Us doubters questing, point by point forestalled;
We were informed that you, degenerate,
Embraced the follies of a warrior's lot,
Turning your back on sweet, preceding ties—
On Iphigenia, callous, reckless you!
Thus here I am (with spies besetting near
At every corner), issues waiting soon
In execution dread, 't is known not what.
'T is terror maketh women doubly feel,
So distant from their palace and their home!

   Achil. There must misunderstanding be in this.
Yet blame not Agamemnon thou for all.
He may complot some triumph to adorn.
Hold fast to love, for love rules men. Be not ·
Infatuated; soon clear-sightedness
Returning, we and others shall rejoice.

   Clyt. He sins by fractions, others helping him,
Although the sum his all at times appears.

   Achil. This half excuses him with charity.

   Clyt. Still Iphigenia's welfare stands forth first.

   Achil. Do not I go to rescue Helen held
By Troy's hard terms, opposing life to death?
Would I do less for Iphigenia harmed,
Whose patience hath a voice in pallid looks,
Whose serenity a solace sheds around,
Whose soul alone in absence me inspires?

   Clyt. You well refute what was alleged against
Your faith; and I exult you honor self
With a demeanor of sincerity:
My daughter's safety in it lies.

Achil. There must be in the wind retarding us
At Aulis here an ill reserved for some
Impiety, transgressing covertly. . . .
Ye gods, guile confound, dealing punishment! . . .
Meanwhile I 'll turn to Agamemnon, still
His friend (though deep he is!)—I 'll go to him,
To judge by surface means; and more to know
Endeav'ring, may through knowledge concord make.

Exit ACHILLES.

Clyt. Oh, let him go in ignorance! Alack!
This Helen, renegade, outlives; and she,
More dear, allegiant e'er, to save her dies—
Dies Iphigenia, the sacred knife to stain;—
Her father's sentence, judging as in law
Against his own, with Calchas at the rear
In arch-deceiving dexterous—these learn
Let him! There 's more behind—con it let him,
This more;—and thus together all arouse
Shall him to such a fury as to make
The bravest quail; at least, 't is so proposed.
Men managed are through passion stirring them
To do that which defeat serves in the end.

SCENE IV.

AGAMEMNON, ACHILLES *and* IPHIGENIA.

Achil. I come before you bearing that within
Which you accusing still excuses you;
My ear would justify your words, your course,

Your semblance late (not social to converse
As wont with some), in hearing you unfold.
Your wife impassioned, suffers and upbraids.
Your Iphigenia here; why is it so
To tread upon the thorny path of war?
Aga. She comes within the shadow of a storm;
The sun, dispersing clouds, shall glorify
The dim beginning in the shining end.
Achil. Her presence here, is it connected with
The object of our expedition stayed?
Aga. It is. Late the local divinity
Consulting Menelaus, Ulysses, I,
With sacrifice upon her altar, heard,
With an authoritative voice, proclaim
To us this Calchas, prophet, what assured
Shall be, with instance that the future brought
Within the circle of the present—he
So potent was! Diana pacified
Must be, demanding richly, as befits
An immortal. Offending much I must
Atone—the stag she favored fell by these
My hands. Question no more, but Calchas seek.

Exit ACHILLES.

Oh, peace departed, left behind in Argos,
Refusing to transmarine shores to go!
Now struggles that, heart-rending, lading with
The dust, make choke the atmosphere of sense,
O'erwhelming are! . . . He will know all, and that,

Too, holding gratitude's indebtment o'er;
For him I owe much, valiant Achilles.
But how is this?—a thought so trammeling
Leads back to childhood, confessing dread
Of him returning. I should dread him not,
And yet I do. His qualities endowed
Have strong and noble touches, fit to bear
The rod of fortitude in cold behalf
Of duty asking that himself be ruled:
Let Calchas so dispose his earnestness!

Enter IPHIGENIA.

What, daughter, here alone! Expected not,
Yet thou dost come fulfilling to a wish,
With flush on cheek, composure on thy brow.

Iph. My father, dear, I yield to you—to that
Which claims you most, superior to the self
That dwells in flesh;—and I no less accede
To Calchas kind yet stern, a votary
Upon the current of decree severe
To be borne, worthy of Minerva's blessing.

Aga. Think not in error of myself I spoke,
With mind distorted from affection just,
Cold in embraces of illusions wild,
To lead thee on, forever from this life
Delivered up. An early innocence
Came forth, as if in mist inspirited,
From days agone, and woke those sentiments
That charmèd me when thou, upon my knee
(Arises clear thy infant ecstasy

E'en now in imagery!) wast then in figure
Invested with the traits of beauty—saw
A woman standing firm in qualities,
Myself reflected in their excellence—
And shook my locks in giddy pride of thee.
Much more, in tenor of this vein, might say
I now, but such avowal would be turned
Awry in serving motive that forbids
Details. To van of thought to forward right
I owe, it making be from wrongs of state
By barbarians, by kings iniquitous;
From overflowing tides of darkness deep,
The guide ideal. Thus consecrated, I
Would to my aim my Iphigenia win,
Judging her death as bliss beyond the tomb.

Iph. I kneel, my father, as I have implied,
Unto the altar's doom, as if a gate
It were, to me alone, to Olympus.

SCENE V.

ACHILLES *and* IPHIGENIA.

Achil. From Calchas I have bitter tidings heard.
Thou dedicated to the altar's rite!
What painful riot in the temper plays!
Dost thou consent?—Ah, me! thy looks are pale.

Iph. Duty a golden medium is to joy.

Achil. Reply of thine it seemed would be just so.
'T was deemed that thou of me forgetful art.
Thy eye's familiar is some vision strange.

Iph. Be thou of bravery thine aware to aid
The will in this emergency imposed.

Achil. 'T is little thee to shield commanding thou;
Patroclus mine (a friend to might and valor)
And the Thessalian host would rescue thee.

Iph. Use arms against the judgment seat, upheld
By motive in the sphere of spheres! No, no!

Achil. Alas, to list! How Calchas' counsels foil!
Now hard to undergo this double trial,
Thy father foiling, too—adverse to that
Late pledge uniting thee to me! Too soon
This in the dust must under foot be crushed!

Iph. It is unjust to speak of this bygone.

Achil. In much I am undone. In what is said
'T is not the choice, but the compulsion speaks.

Iph. Remember Agamemnon's realm of Greece
Is fairest; Iphigenia, princess born,
His daughter, proud of him, of country, too,
Will serve them both in yielding to the claim
Of Diana—country, patriots, father, all
Subserved—what obligation with a meed!

Achil. But such a tenor in her delicacy
Is the advice of chance unsteadiness,
Or human not—so armed against her friends!

Iph. The Parcæ with a vigor have instilled
This frame (that might bear wrinkles and decay) so
To order and ordain their purposes.
Musing of it, what noble feelings stir!

Achil. Shall now forego, Iphigenia, that heart,
In which those noble feelings are, my own,

Keeping in view no resolution proud
Averse to me, but winning maidenhood?
Ah, me! regard that state forlorn of life,
Thy mother's, and thy lover's, too, anon
When thou art gone, thy shade with alien shade
To roam, ne'er to return to earth again!

 Iph. Arousing thus, a spark within myself
Effects the more the cause with thee. But know
A father's wisdom stands a daughter's less
In error's mesh to aid. Inclined to veer
From fixed devotion to her land, her elders,
Her worship at the fane, prohibits she
To entertain thy plea with humbleness;
Nor murmur shouldst thou vain from me estranged.

 Achil. What lot to supplicate without amends!
How doubt belief did! Charlatan was this
Belief in feigning thou didst feign; but truth
Comes through thy features, virtue's seal thereon.

 Iph. Regard profound with suasion would prevail.

 Achil. So speaking seems as if a statue speaks;
It makes the present poor, unfortunate.

 Iph. The future richer by privation now.

 Achil. Still stay! For beauty liveth sternness yet,
Meet due from man. Death tempting thee away,
From this to turn to cold eternity!

 Iph. Aye, aye, there majesty immutable,
Forever cold to those who feel it not.

 Achil. To flutter o'er oneself with spirit brave
Is that unreal in mortals which oft falters when
Comes experience dread. A preceptor

Let pausing moments be. Too soon regretting,
Rash acts anticipate retrieving steps.

Iph. Why thus accost my fear? Why not my faith?
Hallow the gods the tidings fraught for us.

Achil. We cannot praise the gods for all they do;
Then what they bid why sanction always we?

Iph. In candor mine find not a mind amiss,
Void of what claims esteem for intellect.
I would live! Life engenders life, joy joy,
Hope hope. Would I achieving these in lot
To gratify, relinquish it to fade
Ere ripe—to meet in summer autumn's blight—
Without inducing effort stirred within,
Supple and strong as is the palm, to take
A course of rigor that e'en frailty charms?
The gods do surely blunder not in this.

Achil. Oh, so to express!—so unlike the one—
The Iphigenia fair, of earth, for earth,
Adorning and adorned!—so like the one
On a tribunal citing principles!
Retire, at least, in memory; be absent from
These places, in thy native haunts; recall
Thy father, simple there, sweet manners bidding,
Aspiring and unruly not. O'erlooked
That father is; this father, mounting where
He would, sees less and less his wife and children,
Until they are mere ciphers to himself.

Iph. Why should I be a victim to design
When me admonishes clear consciousness
To be steadfast in that I do? What false,

My father! No, no! He for me grieves more
Than I that am to suffer. Faith him knows
As it knows self—as woman knows the depth
Of man, self-knowledge his in instinct naught.

Achil. 'Tis hard to deafen what affection urges
Resigning thee for aye in one dull thought.
Can this accomplished be in so short time?
Profoundest functions of the mind rebel.
Give hours for such, they cycles would appear.

Iph. Oh, court not languor fatal to the sense
That boasts the hardihood of Grecian brawn!

Achil. Still recollection must, corroding this
Same sense, prevail, with age untimely blending—
Sad plight!—a weight upon the manhood's prime,
Making imperfect what encouraged bears
E'en brawn unto the dangerous verge of deeds.

Iph. The end behold! This passion for the present
A poison is, a toil, an ignorance.
Let flowery thoughts be o'er it victory,
Communing with the future as in prayer.

Achil. Yet feel it rue that one so good should leave!

Iph. The grim, gaunt ferryman, of whom we note,
Conveys not, wrapped in terror of his mien,
All numbers vain across the turbid flood.
Beyond, in the abode of all the just,
Associations are enriching to the soul
In tranquil proportions. Of them reflect
To animate belief that now would die;
And that alive in strength would cast the form
Of Iphigenia—thy Iphigenia!—

Into the clasping of fatality,
Deeming it weal. . . . Ah, me! what music were
Thy accents, Achilles—my Achilles!—
Unto my maiden diffidence, that wooed
In harmony obedience to thy nods!—thy smiles,
How vital to expectation in days
Gone by!—my strength with thine so marvelous;
How it made grow, its breath of power through me
As April's through a tree's fresh foliage!
But now I stand at variance with all this,
As breeze that favored late the blossom's birth,
Now changed its bearings, chills it to the core;
Nor blame aught me. Is mercy gone from love
Of thine that nurtured me? Mayhaps 't is masked
Behind the ardor of a warrior's brow
To show again. If so, to plead were idle;
For mercy apprehending will adapt
Itself unto the burden of my plight,
And try to lessen it. . . . O Achilles!
Request no more. Remember prophecy,
Thee auspicious. Thy shade of vagueness turn
To sunshine, wishing what of moral worth
It holds, foreseeing and receiving grace.
The footprints of our day outlast us shall.
Let 's part, each moving in a course aright:
Thou to the fray, I to the tomb, life's foe
In both—my sacrifice first coming moulds
The cause of things; thy sacrifice effect,
Crowning with aweless sword the fall of Troy.

SCENE VI.

AGAMEMNON, CLYTEMNESTRA *and* IPHIGENIA.

Clyt. These galleys that lie idle on the beach;
These sailors that seek foreign shores for sport,
Let the wind-ruler, Æolus, refrain
To aid! Why complicate a spirit base
With what moves majesty, and call both good,
Finding in chance all self-authority?
Iph. Mother, put no such question now, so near
The time to spread light from a dark event.
Clyt. I saw them to the altar go just now
With odored offerings. When thou wast born
No altar was adorned; then innocent;
But guilty now, condemned, misused, disowned,
They must, as if atoning for neglect,
To mitigate the scene, thus honor thee.
Iph. Ah, mother, please refer no more as this!
Let that thee hold, each function loyal e'er,
To the sad covenant my father holds.
Clyt. The skill of Orpheus would him move not.
What cares he for that baleful Helen flown?
What cares she to come back, with Paris fain,
Having, o'er Tyrian garments rare, a chain
Of woven gold around his princely neck?
Why meditate a good to gild an ill?
For she, returning, will pollution bring.
Her beauty bearing 'fore the Trojan dames,

She lives for it, proud, blind to Menelaus.
With rustic vigor born, love's opposite,
He talks of cheeses, goats and herds of beeves!

Iph. Aught overwhelms with silentness; it comes
Upon the air, subduing passion full
To fade, forecasting it to blend with some
Remote contingency, until we have
A mood that stands above a mortal plane
Prepared to die. O mother! do not try
To alter what in me determines so,
Lest thou, incurring ire of what, unnamed,
Unknown, behind me moves, shouldst be in range
Of shaft destructful from on high. So stir
Thy words, that would mislead, for thee and thine
I tremble as a bark sea-struck. Oh, cease!

Clyt. I cannot—thou, a daughter, bidding such!
Thy zeal hath it still not a tie to her
Who gave thee being?—thou, persistent in
A willfulness, resolvèd so to go
Among thy kind, as foreign to my bosom
As to thy neighbor! . . . I distracted am!
I would to Jupiter appeal; believing not,
What must I do? . . . Flow, eyes! regardless weep
Of that desire which would have hardness shield—
The vent maternal of my bitterness!

Enter AGAMEMNON.

Aga. My wife, repress thyself. O'erhearing thee,
Thy language hearing shocked. Speak not in strain

Impious of the father of the gods,
Lest harm betide. Calchas hereafter sees,
Reporting what is best, concealing much,
This best to be repeated in the much
A thousandfold enchained in fixed results.
This I believe. Then, helpmeet, fail not me.

Clyt. If to this outrage now assenting I,
Can I with love uphold as husband you
In years of future, musing of this day?

Aga. Ah, yes; forgetful of thyself, thy mind
In peace shall know 't is sacrilege to stand
As thou dost now, and love thy husband more.

Clyt. Our son Orestes, what shall he be taught
In this?

Aga. The truth; nor grudge the teacher freedom;
Say what he will, it matters not if true.

Clyt. O self! surrender to thy lord. What must
Be will support its right, and consequence
Acquit the doer. Now, ye thoughts, prepare
To an influence exterior to bend;
For know that no interior might could make
Ye alter so. It seems a touch without
Approaches consciousness, adjusting it
To form anew; perceiving much (in gloom
Before) in light disclosing now, it moves
Concordant with that which you would exact.

[*Aside.*

Words! words! for him, but not the aim of them.

Aga. Rejoiced I hear, O wife of Sparta, this!
Seeing to that we plan in vain, 't is well

Death is an ever open portal through
Which to celestial haunts men triumphs bear,
From what they are hereon much raised therein. . . .
So perfectly, with heart so manifest,
Not knowing she of that our league admires,
Hath Iphigenia prompt addressed herself
Unto the full adoption of my choice
(Demurring though at first, susceptible
To fitful fears), she stands in calm relief,
A thing to flatter pride in us paternal.
With Spartan worth, stern quality inborn,
She shineth through the smoke of sacrifice! . . .
Iphigenia, belovèd now as e'er,
Approaches step by step the Hour to take
Thee to the sombre dwelling of the dead;
Art thou, as formerly, as satisfied
To go, subjected to the augury?

    Iph. I am. Let me proceed to pay the debt
My father owes. Myself no longer am
A subject of a birth, its sequels close
Extending to bereave. . . . Vitality,
Delusion's nurse! now mitigate each grief
Attending moments soon to ruin thee. . . .
I have felt that I would not you unveil.
Hence, my frail ghost, the image of a being
Confined, would move forth, as mild Hermes bent
On journey high, impatient to foretaste
The weal ethereal; would yearn, beyond
Exempt from all the flesh's ministry,
In distant periods to expatiate.

Then youth in me must with sad cypress not
For crown, but leaves of joyful laurel, bid
A self-farewell. Death is the heart of life.
Then to the scene, as if a heifer from
The herd, with gilded horns and dew-kissed flowers,
Conduct my feet. Would consecrate this flesh
Diana pure; would purge of vagaries
Coming from thought's perpetual mist on mist;
Of dumb reluctance erring in its course;
Of memories inviolate, yet false in view;
Of virgin lamentations burning yet;
Of mortal sins immortal oft across
In Tartarus! . . . Move to the foreordained!
Come, come! start for the altar—father, guide!
To tarry here afflicts the gods with pain.
Thou shouldst be brave. The pallor on thy brow,
Oh, banish it! The color of a chief
Appears more well. . . . My mother dear, thy tears
Are the survivals of that fear 't is hoped
Is dead; let not thy breast them nurture more;
But weep, if weep thou must, for this day past,
Not morrow near. Unto the sacrifice I go;
The army stands encircling to behold;
Calchas awaits, Diana pressing him.
Adieu! adieu! O mother dear! . . . Lead on!

PRIAM, KING OF TROY.

THE PERSONS.

PRIAM, *king of Troy.*
ÆNEAS, *a Trojan leader.*
NESTOR, } *Grecian leaders.*
ULYSSES, }
HECTOR, *son to Priam.*
OFFICER *and others.*

SCENE I.—Troy; the Grecian hosts before it.

PRIAM *alone.*

Pri. The Greeks lie hapless in the tents on plains
Late ringing, that give play to zephyrs now
From bosom of the South. The cry, *To arms!*
To arms! is sleeping in their mouths. Would it
Ne'er waken more, uprising rash against
Our wallèd town—the ornament renowned
Of Phrygia. To overtures of peace
Give ear, O Time!—Oh, favor them as thou
Dost favor genial Mays succeeding months
Of winters fierce!—lest war thy work shall do,
And crumbling turn our towers to the ground:
Be this thy task. Defended by thy laws,
The foe, by Troy's six gates, immures; but show,
O Time! advantage by the flocks, in fields,
At haunts of home, and let him seek it there,
Withdrawn from here where ills offset his gains.
What miss we Trojans, too, opposing might,

By the hap-hazard art of Mars sustained,
Repulse our lot, made smarting more to deem
Hell's sympathy gives boast to victory?
This awe of circumstance without us leaves
Ineffective, dazed, groping as in dark,
Our nature to arouse to light within, that stirs
Sensations just and reason domineers.
Lamenting we behold the dead, to rise
As heroes nevermore: that fire extinct
Which an illumination spread, and showed
Each triumph is its own encomiast;
Now breaks our transport dreaming of it gone.
Why turn to count the waste of numbers soon
As they to fall? This count forecast affords ·
Composure not far darkling on the view
Departing hence. Let day of peace forestall;
Let satisfaction find in this a meed;
Let groves of olive shelter what they grant;
Let shafts of wingèd doom to wingèd doves
Give place. O Time! afford (returning sweet!)
The means conducive to this end, to hold
Despair from its apportionment! . . . Oh, would
This Helen were with Menelaus, and Pride,
The false, the leader to this siege, were where
Humanity a master is! As pupils then
Men would be sages soon, and warriors hold
In execration. . . . Æneas approaches!
He comes on the desire immediate
That would confide in one as safe as he.
                    Enter ÆNEAS.

Hail! hail! brave bearer of the shield. The news
From the besiegers' ground relate if well.

Æne. Not well for them; for us, perhaps, 't is so.
Their sentinels are scorched upon the rounds.
Views them with scorn the solitary Sun,
As if he would our cause abet, and lay
Each armèd Greek cold at the feet of Death.

Pri. Let 's follow this advantage to the test
Of more to come. Be you favorable
To what is purposed with your aid. The time 's
Mature for other action than to face
With stubborn brow the foe besetting Troy;
To linger out our days, privations near,
With self-inflictions adding to chagrin,
Waiving that touchstone—happiness. This plight
Unroyal dictates duty to a king;
For grief is wisdom's antecedent school.
Go to the Greeks encamped, as messenger
To speak; Ulysses find; Diomedes;
Or Nestor (nearest Agamemnon's ear,
The chief of chiefs), his eloquence to warm
Propitious to ourselves;—to them say all
(If fortune so allow) that Priam, not
For partiality, but equity,
With honor quests the terms of equal peace.

Æne. I would, O king! yet would I not. Consent
Would go, but tarries confidence. I am
A soldier void of tact to harmonize,
With language apt persuasive to a point,
Discordant men. To plead is better than

My tongue my sword. Why not leave Antenor
Be substitute in this affair? He is
Without a peer when an occasion calls
For promptitude to advocate a cause,
Failing not to attain whereby to thrive
Betime when others fail endeav'ring more.

 Pri. Antenor's prized; but less by me when choice
Requires the self-dictates to meet the form
Of unexpected things. Your traits, though few,
Are sturdy, fitting for the hour, the place
To bear upon them what would weigh his down;
Your speech sufficient, and your prudence just.
Thus talented, refuse not me the task
I would have you now undertake for Troy.

 Æne. Refuse I not, O king!—outright, at least.
But recollect the Greeks have craft, and I
Have none; that they have art, and I have none;
That they have wit, and I have none. A host
Himself Ulysses is, unmatched, renowned:
Yet who, to gain his point (so is it said),
Within the circle of ambition fair
Moves not; but lurks without, adept, for prey
Lynx-eyed. There Nestor is, whose eloquence
Is music's instrument, inspiring foes
To turn to friends, to cast their cause behind,
To follow where he leads, adversely moved
Against their own. There's Achilles proof-hard;
Contrary, though reserved; insidious, too,
With motives various—now for love, and now
For strife;—with lusty voice he reasons not,

But roars his passion out. Confront I must
A willfulness most thrifty in excuse,
For service in its own behalf,
Of these; yea, yea, by others, to themselves
Law-givers, judging harshly, guile of theirs
At work to flourish ever, must stand I
Surrounded, balked, by them sent back to you
A Trojan scorned. To meet and turn against
Themselves with that they 'd cumber me—to fetch
The olive branch away—the firm address,
The winning use of words from feeling free
(So e'er promotive of an issue good!)
Of Antenor will better serve. On him,
In view of this and much unsaid, still known,
I pray, the duty be conferred at once.
   Pri. No, no! It is imperative for you to go,
With favors antidoting enmity.
Hence let consent move hand-in-hand with what
Is bid; with what requires that self should be
Behind, design before, absorbed in earnestness
Well to acquit itself. Thus 'mong the Greeks,
What presence for a safeguard, bearing down
Each spell opposing! 'T is the spirit true,   ·
Diplomatic, moves to success ill-placed;
For men subdued by means sincere, and led
To grant, approving what they do as that
Proceeding from themselves, are wont to grant
With double bounty. Furthermore, the gods,
Observing you, with mission just, will prompt
A speech and method suited to prevail.

Hence halt not; let the soldier's courage be,
To act, unto the envoy's caution joined.

Æne. I cease to argue. I as soldier yield
To commandment. The Grecian leaders found
Shall hear that Priam, king of Troy, asks truce,
Whereby to sound the chords of peace—the harp
In hand, the trumpet laid aside. Returned,
Relate will Æneas outcome with them.
Proceeding thus, accomplished be your orders?

Pri. Aye, aye! Depart. Let seemly haste impel.
Hereafter come again with news joy-bearing.

Exit ÆNEAS.

SCENE II.—In the Grecian camp.

ULYSSES, NESTOR *and* ÆNEAS.

Ulyss. Nestor, awake! let not the sluggard's tent
Your wisdom shade; within, its tempting fold
Deprives to view of pictured excellence,
Which on the citadel of Ilium
Hangs now in mists. Aurora's aerial tints
Are cast with rosy fingers wet in dawn.
Your taper's restless flame should smoke you out.
Come, come, man! breathing exercise yourself!

Enter NESTOR.

Nest. O comrade, hail! Now what is felt is not
Of me, but me conveyed as largess from

The fount of Life, reviving morn by morn.
Now worship coincides with what is best
Derived from sleep, approach so near to that
Which is a summons to existence's close.

Ulyss. We hear too oft this strain of casual talk;
Of pious theories; of portents many,
Keen to anticipate, false in results.
Deluding self, you others would delude.
Why a soothsayer be to deal in kind,
Discoursing of Mount Ida's store of gods;
Of Scamander, and her reputed nymphs;
Of mystagogues, traversing from afar
To bother us (save entertaining you!)
And not a soldier with his antic airs,
Prating, with themes off-hand, of what our league
Should magnify, respite from war unsought?
What recks— . . . But who is yon advancing here?
Ho, ho, a nondescript! to seek your tent,
I swear, with an outlandish gibberish
Attention to excite: what means to use
For Troy's downfall; what indicate to him
A bird's entrails; his so-forths and so-forths
Gathering volume in sonorous flow! . . .
Seriously, half afraid he straggles here;
If worth he have, 't is of the modest sort
That women like. A shepherd he, perhaps,
Leaving his flock, with what across his shoulders
A wolfish hide appears. Still is his look
Mysterious, and augurs much that fear
Confounds with truth, the heart uncertain what

To feel, the mind what to believe. . . . But, no!—
Doth vision fail, forsaking me? It is,
On closer view, no renegade from Troy,
But a commander late confronting us.
What wants he here among antagonists?
'T is Æneas, upon my word, disguised!
    Nest. Beware of him! He seeks what we should
        hold;
Yet let us listen him with due reserve,
Not cold, lest freezing him it may deter
The candor that confides in deference.
    Ulyss. Advise you well, O comrade! Him accost
Let me. Behind step where the tent obscures;
There hearing wait the consequence of what
His answers make to questions put. Meanwhile,
As if upon cross-purpose bent, I 'll stir
Him so that if deceit he bear, it will
Be shown in contradiction. Hasten in!
He comes a seeming prowler to this place.

       Exit NESTOR. *Enter* ÆNEAS.

    Æne. Is this Ulysses, king of Ithaca?
    Ulyss. It is. What man are you?
    Æne.   Æneas I.
I issued from the gate of Troy ere dawn.
    Ulyss. Why hither come so venturesome to stand?
I tremble for your fate if known by here
To Grecian hosts a Trojan leader is—
A hue and cry, and murder with a sling!
    Æne. The gods beheld with fear, I fear not death.

Ulyss. What credence can I give to this in guise
Of shepherd you, to come so awkwardly
Misgiving us? Is it for espionage
That you are here? You will for answer give
A *no;* but how am I to trust this *no*
When you convicted are before insight
Of stepping on our grounds unworthily?

Æne. I do not wear this habit to mislead;
It is to signify the shepherd's lot—
The virtue mothered by the hills, wild flowers
Among, with bleating lambs by ewes—the crook,
And not the sword. From Priam I, who sends
His greeting. His decision on the throne
Is this, to proffer you the olive branch.
He would have me hold speech with all your chiefs;
Would know if strife by their insistence must
Pursue a bloody course. . . . Oh, hear my cause
With trust!—if void of faith, you me undo.

Ulyss. Our chiefs are scattered here and there;
Some in pavilions loll, whilst others roam.
They bear such characters as fail in ease
When terms exacting ask obedience.
Troy rouses rage: why crave we yield to her?
Is Menelaus to find revenge in peace?
What water tame this peace who thirsts for blood!

Æne. O Greek! your valor question none of Troy;
Of this same trait your wisdom is a match:
Oh, let them both my mission turn to aid!
In setting artifice of pride apart,
Let me, a suppliant, be in degree

Much less, my cause much more; thus entertained,
For sake of Greece, for sake of Troy reply!
   Ulyss. A servant of the hour is not my power;
It is the subject of experience long.
Patience, as beast of burden, wrong o'er wrong
Of Troy sustained. As beacon lights, that glow
From mount to mount, the news ran wildly far:
Paris the climax caps! The thought was dire:
Barbarous Trojans coming to our homes,
And then outraging them—proud Greece, renowned
For civil polity, from Phrygia,
Half knowing laws, corrupt, to tolerate
Her deed! Now do you wonder anger rose,
Inspiring shame, then power with triple strength,
Aggressive to maintain what us is due,
To move, my host and I, from Ithaca, ..
Here to avenge sad Menelaus? Deem you
Our bosom's zeal, with heat burned out, must show
A bed of ashes? No, burn on it must,
At last involving ruin flames to spread.
Think you, the brave commander of our troops
Must turn to Priam changed in mood because
Troy would not have spears hostile in her clime?
Think you, must we return to Greece, our wives
To guard, forgetting Helen left behind,
Each Trojan visitor alert to dupe?
   Æne. Helen, alas! of woes so manifold
The cause, is not integral to the part
Concession would hold back. . . . But to detail
Of armistice I am permitted not

To move; the king direct alone there goes.

Ulyss. What is averred believing all is vain.

Æne. Then bear my speech, the best and worst—
The grain and chaff—to Agamemnon (me
Denied), the chieftain of ye leaders all,
Who may befriend its worth, its dross ignore.

Ulyss. Humph! Agamemnon is too near akin
To Menelaus to give reception fair
To what you offer here. His brother would
Its virtue vitiate, confusing it
With shrewd make-shifts suggested by the wound
He bears, inflicted by his consort held.

Æne. To deem this Helen soon to be restored
Should cause him joy; thus mollified, he would
By nature's feelings urged, to overture
From Troy concede a share of patronage.
What policy for him, and fame likewise,
Before invading hosts, so fortified
In fortitude, its limit to announce,
Rewarding conflicts past with peace! peace! peace!

Ulyss. It will take time to temper heat in men,
Impassioned, counting not the sands of life,
To gain the final victory, with song
Hymenean (as if it marriage were,
Venus favoring it), to greet the glad event!

Æne. Alas, too true! emotions lead, and false!
Nevertheless, O Greek! yourself persuade
To yield to sentiment, arising o'er
Past wrongs, that bids cessation of armed feud.
O Greek! if so, you fellow-chiefs instill,

Tending to wake them to impressions bent
As yours, and soothing to perplexity. . . .
Awaiting your disposal of this case,
I go. Troy stands immured, authority
Tenacious of; withal, the olive branch
One hands upholds, the other grasps the sword.
Oh, let the sword fall low, the branch prevail!

Exit ÆNEAS.

Ulyss. He goes, a lion bayed! Within himself
He bears the spirit not of peace; he feels
Too much. A torment such as his must vent
Itself to ease the mind in some gross act.

Enter NESTOR.

Nest. He stood so pillar-like against your words,
Showing the hero through and through! Alas,
Such one should be conjoined against our ranks!

Ulyss. You favor him. He's plausible. Does he
Not wear the wolfish hide, attracting thus
Suspicion on himself? I feel his steps
To follow would be caution to denote
His presence is dishonored by distrust.
His mien was as a cur's, to reconcile
Him to a master who offended stands;
But as he warmed in speech, he shone above
His minor self, superior as a man
In that false way dissimulation holds,
That would enlighten if it could, for it
Should, urged and tasked by high authority.

4 - D

Nest. One-sided you. You weigh with scales
That ever favor self. 'T is well to try
His case as one complex. To claim to know
Him all is to transcend that which is well.
The gods of knowledge false in us make sport,
And us confound to punish for conceit.

Ulyss. That 's so; yet error holds some truth as salt
That seasons oft the mental pabulum:
What taste likes well belief finds proof for it.
Æneas' evidence against himself
Is such as reason obvious moves to deem.
Good-will to him forbids not e'en this right;
Misgiving just passed by, ignored, unheard,
Is duty held in thrall. We soldiers here
Must guard our safety in defense, that asks
That done which, counter to the spirit's choice,
Must grossly labor to avert the aims
Of those who, through deceiving, would attain
Some point of victory. Æneas thus
I fear. He is a warrior blunt and bold;
But as a man a fox in circumstance
And stratagem. He goes to Priam now
To breathe those feelings by the throne which make
Kings move purblind 'gainst fate, their satellites
To blame, in mischief working for themselves.

Nest. Yet if he came in all sincerity
To help restore the peace, what follows now
Your bluff reception must be wrong from you.
Within himself now much displeasure reigns,
Perhaps. 'T is well to ask, who placed it there?

The mere imprudence of your course may turn
Advantage from our side in battle pitched,
The gods befriending his, the Trojan's side.
In just accord he with supernal laws;
Excite Fate's enmity at fault ourselves.

Ulyss. How variable! You cried at first: *Beware*
Of him! He seeks what we should hold. Why now
Condemn the language used, as you in part
Impelled its strain? . . . In danger here we are,
For Nestor stands engend'ring such a plight!
Affected must we be by that *he* urges! . . .
Does Priam send him here from Hector's side
(Who is so open, imposition scorning),
Or from the couch of Paris, timorous,
Yet heartless, cunning, Helen's paramour?
Of these two sons the father Priam is:
'T is safe to judge by offspring of the king,
Whose evils mingled are with virtues clear.
If fraught with honor he, why herald it
Through such as Æneas, arriving here
With dubious movement, honor's counterpace?

Nest. Paris o'erlook awhile; Hector mark:
A statue not empowered less than he
Imposes and retains the feelings to itself,
Rousing heroic thoughts. The sire, indeed,
Must be a certain portion of the son,
Who honor shows, old Priam's gift, who moved
Himself thereby Æneas sent to us.

Ulyss. But did this Priam say to Æneas
(His honor bootless 'gainst the heat of rancor),

Take you this hide of wolf, and, wearing it,
Go seek our enemy and sue for peace,
With inner motive hid and treacherous?
Thus Paris shows in him, not Hector frank.
But if this Æneas acted thus alone,
Moved to impress us with a kind effect,
Seeking to win with worthy means, these means
Have proved with flaw, and we have right to choose
A harsh occasion to rebuke his plea,
And answer, too, thereby, the king of Troy.

    Nest. The times give joyless nursing to the senses;
He came on us in our predicament.
Our armies are seditions hatching late;
They bear the hardships of a siege prolonged—
The bafflings, throes from nameless maladies—
And murmur for their home. Hence you, fatigued
With crowding under foot conspiracies,
Maintain not that reflective poise by which
To judge serenely of an opponent,
That would by his own choice change to a friend.

    Ulyss. That is, apparently. 'T is Nestor trusts.
I see more keenly with a spirit roused;
Salvation comes through human eagerness.
I may amiss behold true Æneas;
But in beholding wisdom much enjoins.
Besides, it seems that Priam pressed to yield
By some exhaustion must surrender soon;
And that for us to show a tendency
To shrink would waive a right for us to say
To what conditions should comply his course.

This idea tempered passion as I spoke
To Æneas, as otherwise to him
I might have been more rude. 'T is left to you,
My method reading in this light, to judge—
Opposed the stand to Æneas; attained,
The bearing of the end; the theories
To be observed by Greece, Troy's foe; the scheme
Of conquest to secure redemption's store;—
Of these judge you, and me acquit of blame.

SCENE III.—In Troy.   Priam's palace.

PRIAM, HECTOR, ÆNEAS, OFFICER *and* HERALD.

Hect.   You ask me to submit to these demands;
To favor peace from yonder Greeks, resolved,
Ingenious in resentment stemmed, to bear
Themselves above ourselves; to yield anon
To Menelaus this Helen, repelling all
Our brother's right to her.   Let Paris speak
In this.   For me, desire to satisfy
Ambition with the deeds of courage born
Is first.   For her, the queen, no sentiment
Should come between the course of holding her,
Or of releasing her, to hinder us
From driving one by one the foe, o'erwhelmed,
Their only safeguard Greece, their mother land.
Beleaguer us (their vaunt!) not long in vain;
A certain justice strained their cause supports;
Influenced thus, their spirit is unapt

To cede meet dues to us in intercourse,
So double in endeavor to o'erreach e'en friends,
We Trojans less would trebly be them prey.

Pri. Our profit not is in revenge; it is
Not sanctified by Heaven; imbitters what
It eats, and thirsts as Tantalus. Besides,
Our plains should bear for harvest gilded sheaves,
Not bristling spears and battle-axes sharp;
Those to sustain our life, these to destroy.

Hect. I am most dutiful as son to you;
From youth to man was taught I reverence
For rules particular, wherein my steps
Have followed as a path, gave ease to use
And love to habit, that to break in part
Therefrom is self-regard impaired, somewhat
Of penalty; but duty can exist
In opposition's plea, and laurels gain
In license. Therefore me a pardon grant
In saying Hector does concealment spurn,
In justice to his sire, in leading him
Believe he stands with silence to agree
In this so moving him. To conquer now
Is progress; to succumb, it to impeach;
A zigzag lapse to take, amiss at last
To be as bondsmen, shamed and portionless.

Pri. 'T is pride inborn conceives a specious vista;
Your mother's hauteur ever bides with you.
The future certain, graphic, zeal reproaches;
'T will show surmises past deceptive webs
Whereon were wingèd fancies caught. To threat

The present stands with danger, fashioning
Disasters odious, chief victims ours.
Hence caution should control experience,
That bids the patriot relinquish much;
That leads him seek sedate philosophy,
Vexation's balm, adapting ends to ends.

Hect. But why should courage not exert itself
To bring about such things as sages cheer,
E'en to a point decisive to attain
Whereby to yield is plain necessity?
Then to submit is satisfaction's part
To soften what our foemen would impose,
In deeming that exhausted are the means
Which strove, fulfilling not success, but that
Which gives to failure honor's ornament.

Pri. Now sore of mind, such things discomfort it.
A course has been determined on to serve—
That would make short the interval between
The seed and fruit. Æneas sent hath been
Into the Grecian camp, there to confer
With the commanders; to suggest that Troy
Will at the rites of peace administer.
Returning he may issues bring that must
Be met not with reluctance, shifting from
The scene; not with bravado, wrong and scornful—
Impulses of a warrior. . . . Oh, let
The gods decree that instantly descend
Inspiring all serenely to the means
Subservient to our kingdom's interest!

Enter Æneas.

Welcome once more, the leader of my hosts!
The mud your ankles bear is proof enough
A servant comes, e'er dutiful, our cup
To sweeten. . . . What to you the Grecians said?
Are they inclined to wage still 'gainst our walls,
So stubborn, fury stubborn of their own,
Or to depart from Phrygia for home,
There to partake repose, denied them here?

   Æne. I to Ulysses spoke of your desire.
To a fixed station of unbending thought
He moved, then language used implying that
As suitor I was vain. I felt so curbed,
Spoke cowardice as in a beggar's limbs,
As he, more proud than e'er, half looked at me.

   Pri. Alas, and you so honest in your motive!

   Æne. Finally, thinking of your wish for peace,
I intimated what to it might add
In value much that woke within my mind,
That deeming probable you would concede
To them, the Greeks, in order to induce
Him well to hear my case. My manners changed,
Impelled by the occasions of ordeal,
Beyond what patience taught an hour before,
And moved my mission to accuse itself
Ill done. Ulysses then, erroneous,
An opposition took such as to quote
Its verbal course would not be profiting
Unto ourselves. Enough is said, I left
Him fixed against the realm's security
In that degree as to assail, he yearns,

It to a downfall. But with time's own change,
His views must change; and cooled, they may avail
Themselves of what is better, and advance
To where I would have led them to myself.
May Heaven, that guides our days, so favor us!
    Pri. Meanwhile, O Troy! hast much to undergo
From the events that in appearance spring
From earth's fatality, as cursing us
For rising human from her soil! Thus more
And more affairs combine themselves, to plans
Adverse that would calm hours restore. Thus this
And that in opposition stand in man,
E'en from the womb unto the tomb! . . . Hector,
Among our people move; their attitude
Discern toward their government; they much
Now suffer, suff'ring more the cause unspoken,
Close at the heart to canker. But, alas,
'T is sad to counsel ears as thine! Thou art
In contravention to my wish (Troy's weal),
And farther would it separate from right
To wrong. . . . I humbly turn, O Æneas!
To thee, the succor of gray hairs, to feel
Its essence as the flame that warms the limbs
In winter chilled and stiff; withal, to feel
A confidence that, chiding, shows my sons
Reflect the folly of their stock in that
Uncurbed, and learn the lesson of reproach.
    Æne. You should not think so sorely of your sons,
With character abroad rare, prominent,
Where every humble roof their triumphs flatters.

Pri. You flatter, too, in thus excusing them.
But call it melancholy, fond of late
To move me so to feel; beholding, too,
Severe. Withal, 't is hard this enmity
Of men to face, assembled, host by host,
From o'er the briny waters, to avenge
For injury that had origin here,
Our future's name enscrolled in black reproof!
Yet must we, though offenders past, and now,
Despite ourselves, offending still, be bold
Protecting well the fair in us, the gross
Associate a shelter, too, to give. 'T is thus,
Contending with affairs, that men, inclined
To rectitude, do carry inner stain
They blush to name; 't is thus that kingdoms, too,
Have workings in themselves enfeebling much,
That cause, against their nobler quality
(That would control), suspicious realms to rise,
To war inspired, them anxious to destroy.

Æne. You utter truth, O best of Asia's kings!
But recollect the Greeks are at our gates;
You would have them, ignoring much bygone,
Each breach of faith, as pilgrims enter all;
'T is not their choice, alas! What must we do?
The Parcæ, pitiless, direct us not:
From night we must emerge if can to day.
An index be, O king! If to lay down
Our arms—point so; 't is done: or if to bear
Them forth in struggle dire—point so; 't is done.
The men of Troy bow to their sovereign.

Pri. Thus glory comes from such obedience;
To this indebted, I these men owe much;
In them rewarding, Troy should triumph hold.
This idea happy makes to spurn the Greek,
To note the horror he essays to spread,
To deem him worthy of the javelin's doom.

Hect. He comes to humble us, ransack our homes,
Towers o'erthrow, fanes desecrate, retreats
Most holy level, Ilium sacrifice,
Burnished war-cars and all the horses seize,
Lead stalwart men in irons—aye, Oh, you,
The king of men, the sire of fifty sons!
Would harness to a chariot in a realm
To you most strange, its chief to draw before
A populace to greet the victory.
Consider these; not far in time, perhaps,
To be the sharp experience of us all.

Pri. Although excessive this, yet truth it has,
And forcible the likelihood! Still, son,
Could we but mitigate the Grecian rage,
Turn men humane, themselves resigned to reason,
An office then endeavor would encrown
More golden to esteem than this we wear.
Since not our wish for peace is first (that would
To good deeds a light-bearer be), but war
To lead, we must as partial cowards hear
The trumpeters, and follow to the fray,
And bravery prove—yet tremble will each knee.

Enter an OFFICER.

Offi. A herald comes beseeching interview
With you, O king! A message bears his bosom
From the beleaguers, for imperial ears
Alone. He waits without command to hear.
    Pri. His errand to fulfill bid him draw nigh.

Enter a HERALD.

Unburden, man, of what you have for us.
Have no concern for those about, for they
Are such as prize as duty secrecy.
    Her. You to address, O ruler famous! I
Am here from Agamemnon, king of kings.
I bear a challenge from Achilles stern;
Yet not so stern but that affection's spark
His mind inflames, his dear Patroclus mourning;
Who would your Hector, slayer of his foe
(Dead friend to Greece!) encounter soon with arms
In combat single on the plain by Troy.
    Hect. I am so ready I would now be there,
Him to confound, his figure to lay low,
To typify the fall of all his cause.
    Pri. Are you, within your camp, so idle grown
You need the pageant of a fray between
The prince, my son, and him, Peleus' son?
Their blood once spilt, can it atonement serve?
Your rams, why batter more against our walls?
Yourselves, exhaustion's prey, why not sustain?
Your ships, why not with honor quest their shores,
The rowers busy churning ocean to a foam,

The sails inflated, blessed with winds of peace?

Her. You queries follow in an order such
I know not how to answer them, except
To break the obligations that restrain.
From Agamemnon grave I come, O ruler!
His gravity, his silence much forbid,
And long example holds in loyalty.

Hect. Yes, go to him, and say accepted is
The challenge; say, besides, the son of Priam,
In panoply, will Achilles confront
Between the city and your smoking camp.
The day, to-morrow name, at trumpet's note,
Issued upon the citadel, Ilium.

Her. I go to Agamemnon to convey
Your words, O prince! . . . Adieu, O king!

Exit HERALD.

SCENE IV.—In the Grecian camp.

ULYSSES *and* NESTOR.

Ulyss. Achilles soon will signify to all
His prowess o'er the lusty, handsome prince,
Hector, who towers despite antagonism
Above what Grecian eyes would see in him.

Nest. The dawn's birth-note comes; scenes radiant
Refresh; their colors ample mists unfold,
As if by river-nymphs bedight. This day
What contrast gory must assoil! That speech

Of Æneas so orders thoughts they would
Prevail to honor what it bore, on him
Reflecting thus a beauty luminous.
His voice had wisdom, though we heard it little;
After-effect its echo is with charm to woo.
Oh, would soon end this campaign wearisome!

    Ulyss. To tend aloof from what you have avowed
Is your profession now, at variance next
With this to plead for war! . . . Time-serving, prone
To show a gift of eloquence, it leader,
He follower, is Nestor's soft example! . . .
Would you have Achilles turn from himself,
As you, give way to Troy, outrages past
And others yet condone, a downward step
Pursue, as man ascending nevermore?

    Nest. Ulysses, know the Greeks example are
To all surrounding people of the earth,
E'en to its edge where ocean shows no more;
Know this example flawed, is moral power
Descending, going to the glooms below.
Greece should be just as much as friend as foe
To all mankind itself besides: as foe,   •
Attacked, tenacious of its rights; as friend,
Invoked, forgetful of itself, but not
Of law correct, impartial, dealing dues.
The tone of Æneas appeared for this.
All praise to him! . . . This conflict of to-day,
Between their Hector and our Achilles,
Should close in peace: if Hector victor be,
Then Troy should arbitrator stand, but Greece

If Achilles. Of Agamemnon's ear
Let 's seek attention to abet this course.
Our struggle long is struggle's vanquisher,
Us to exhaust by time's dilemmas weaved.

Ulyss. Your mother's nature is too much in you;
Your father's, passive, steals from energy
For war's stern claim that marshals soldiers true.

Nest. It may be so. Still this maternal trait
Of warmth, let Heaven (refined inspirer!) shield!
Ulysses you less hard would be more dear;
The counsels of the soul would stir you more,
Attaching you to men and women, too,
In recognition of life's righteousness
Evolving in the races of the earth.

Ulyss. Tut! tut! such phrases fit not what we are.
To quaver now! Is hardihood to take
The rear of diffidence, whose skulking shadow
Return would home? Evoking rigid measures,
Great war at hand, with terms effeminate
You meet the call—at heart the otherwise
Of what you seemed—the *one* that swore, as o'er
The deep he came, e'en in his throes, sea-sick,
To Neptune's ear, with strokes of battle's skill
The best a path to find for victory,
E'en in the citadel! . . . This truth all know:
Of Priam's lofty town we 'll bend the head!
Ye winds diffuse, this threat bear to Troy's throne!
Ye winds, know, too, by strength or stratagem,
That if or Hector or Achilles dies
To-day our strife in neither death finds end!

SCENE V.—In Priam's palace.

PRIAM, ÆNEAS, OFFICER *and* ORACLES.

Pri. Where 's Hecuba? My wife, my favorite,
Anear should be, her grace to minister.
Offi. She, with the matrons all retired, is gossip
Hearing. They weave, and smile, and sing. Betimes
They change their mood, their theme exploits of men
And demi-gods so long ago on earth;
Of Hercules, the monsters slaying, he
To be no more with mortals, now immortal.
An expectation gloweth through their task,
As hums each spinning-wheel's low monotone.
To hear them oft the senses overtakes
With new-made fire, reviving youth in age.
Pri. 'T is ever thus: men's deeds, however brutal,
Yet modified by fame, are women's praise.
Offi. They talked awhile of one most dear to all,
Whose reputation is the commonwealth's—
The bulwark of the state in days as these.
Pri. Of Hector this. Where is he now? Not here
He comes to know, as wont, his father's bidding.
Offi. I heard a tumult in the street. To know
The cause a messenger in speed was sent,
Who soon returning uttered this in joy:
Brave Hector hath from Andromache gone
To meet Achilles, face to face to fight !
I learned thereafter, from another voice,
Their parting was affecting e'en to tears.

With heavy step she moved alone to mourn;
With buoyant step he moved toward the gate.
Those who, walls posted on, beheld him last
Said he strode on the plain, a prince, indeed!
His plumes high nodding, kissed by zephry Day,
As if to her endeared. . . . . Anon he meets
His opponent in bloody exercise
To vie. Oh, may good fortune him attend!
'T is hard to deem him as a victim marked,
His attributes so in his courage shine!
  Pri. Impulsive, goes he thus! Oh, that he were
As one to calculate the means to win,
And that ignored is courage void of arms!
  Offi. With him the people in elation are:
Their beau-ideal from youth, when first he trode
The thoroughfares of Troy. He grew; surprise
Awakened often was with some display
Of unexpected worth. In consequence,
Their faith goes with his pride, believing that
Destiny it approves. Thus they exclaim:
Great Hector, now all Asia's choice, return
Will soon with glory to enwaft his name
From land to land, a hero for all time!
  Pri. O people whimsical! purblind to plans,
Adjusted to control crowned thrones, of Jove's
Contriving, aspirations fresh with frost
To wither, hesitate, and think, and know
So to exclaim vexatious is to him,
Who over you empowered rules, to hear—

The very prattle of regardless mouths! . . .
I would be, man, alone. Within there steals
A cast of feeling made for solitude;
The mixture, melancholy, drugs each thought.

Exit OFFICER.

I would have succor from the lips of Fate.
The mind a gleam upholds, that shows my life,
A river turbid, left a mother spring
Of purity; it must flow on, by other streams,
Still sullied more, self-anguished by its lot! . . .
Behold! what 's this upon the dusky wall?—
Ghosts roaming, shrouded, silent, horrid all,
As squadrons come and go in dust and din—
The din, how muffled rolling through these halls!
A voice is heard, as if by winds faint borne:
Of Priam's lofty town we 'll bend the head!
Is this an omen for deep purpose sent?
Holds it relation to the fatal truth
Of sure events approaching to embroil?
Better to hope false-wise than to foretell
Reality the present to make sad.

Enter ÆNEAS.

Returned again? Or spectre thou, bereft,
From battle-sounding plains, thy body slain?
Such seems. The air is full of wingèd forms.
   Æne. No, no! If any ghost appears 't is his—
To voice what happened has, what pangs! O gods!

Pri. O Æneas! is Hector sacrificed?

Æne. Indeed, by hand of Achilles. He lies
All bruised, unconscious of the deed
Of Grecian victory, his flesh-life closed.

Pri. Such was the prophecy to moral counsel,
And which, now proved, is reconciled by us
In part because with previous blow it struck;
And, too, because, once here, it master is.
No rampart of the mind prevails against
The subtle energy of sure-set laws,
That steal within, dread presence to control! . . .
O Peace! where art thou now, deserting us? . . .
O Troy! thy walls are but mere stumbling stones,
Thy foes to fall upon, to rise again
More wroth. The night of change thy towers cast,
Now beautiful in day, in ruin shall.
Heaven proclaims: *The Greeks are instruments;*
The gods offended fit the penalty!

Æne. Oh, go no farther thus declaring, king!
There are remaining noble ones to guard
Your person; others, too, of fortitude,
Troy's enemies to front with valiant zeal,
Until, as ashes pale, this zeal 's extinct.
Hector, dear shade, although retired below,
Lives in the ardor of a multitude.

Enter two ORACLES.

Pri. Oh, men, to counterfeit the voice of Time,
Announcing omens that this day refutes!

Did you not both say Hector would survive,
In grandeur clad, the horrors of this siege?
1st Or. I did.   'T was Heaven prompted thus.
For cause unknown it 's altered incidents.
2d Or. That happen shall to give a lucky issue.
Prized Troy's advantage comes from Hector's fate.
Pri. Believe not so, ah me!   Ye oracles,
False pillars of this realm, your words ill-chosen—
Ye tyros (better name!), know Priam saw
This day's misfortune hover o'er, with woes
At hand uniting woes to come.   Witness
Shall ye Troy low at feet of Greece, with wounds
To plant; her throngs (proud, bowed in tears!) led off,
The goad of bondage theirs, to foreign climes;
And Andromache, Hector's widow now
Too soon, by victor-hands, conducted, grieving,
Then princess not, bid spin for boorish strangers,
Her blushes artless confusion to their eyes.
Presaging thus, ye men, by that abstruse,
The vision's mirror facts to come reflects. . . .
Ah, Æneas, prepare thee for the hour!
The closing scene is nigh.   Mayst thou outlive,
An honor now to Jove, more glorious yet!
My path declining is to Stygian wilds.
Adieu! Adieu! seems proper now to utter;
For whitened is the beard upon my chest;
For autumn's gloomy color is at hand;
For pale flocks bleat when frost destroys the flowers.
Hence, Æneas, e'er faithful one, farewell!
In Fields Elysian may we meet again.

ANDROMACHE IN CAPTIVITY.

THE PERSONS.

ANDROMACHE, *widow of Hector.*
PYRRHUS, *king of Epirus.*
KALANTHA, *a confidante to Andromache.*
ORGILUS, *a Trojan bondman.*

SCENE I.—In Buthrotum, city of Epirus.

ANDROMACHE *alone.*

An. It seems come hither they, the dead, from past
Arising. Adversity doth impel
With longings that impart to passing hours
'T is known not what of feelings new to life.
Not what it was is earth; 't is frozen o'er;
Of yore it bore a vestment green with flowers.
Beheld there is a girlhood fresh and joyful;
A wifehood next, by Hector's heart besought,
Adorement his in trusting prodigal.
E'en knew his horses me, approaching, neighing, fed
From these same hands. Those evanescent days,
With moral meaning bound, translated not
By tongue, so woven they are with the mind!
Then when on breast they laid the babe, was felt
Through him, my lord, through him, my son,
Thence through his issue, joined to glory of
My land, my Troy, my shrine, my home. No bird
More fond than I of what made love confiding.

But love, unstable, leaveth nature false
In this, I would be other than I am;
And true in this, I would be rather what
I was, brave Hector's bride! A captive mourning,
Condemnèd to desire to cheer these hours
With the vague hope, enamored once again,
To rise by love to love's superior lot
Before enjoyed, in that the wish makes fear,
Fear grief, grief double torment to one bound.

Enter PYRRHUS.

Pyr. Why so soliloquize? Your words o'erheard
In part, bid me believe you are at war
With some interior passion broke afresh.
Is it a struggle 'gainst events that rise?
If so, they shape; they wound; they heal, for time 's
Their remedy, physician to events;
But if 't is passion hidden, bitter to
Your peace, rebels, conceal it not, lest growing
Stronger it may oppress—a tyrant then:
Free speech its foe, the friend of liberty.
An. My spirit haunts a sphere unknown to men—
Most all to you. A woman's heart 's unread
As nature's is. Pardon this speech. . . . My lost,
Where are they now? You stand between my own
(That are with likeness memory's scenes within)
And me—*that* is the passion moving much
You heard. A widow aching answers thus,
When things so near the soul are half revealed.

Pyr. Alas, thus to express oneself! At times
You are above refined, but now below.
Are measured not aright we Grecians here
In deeming they you trammel with distrust,
Retaining friendly favors from your state
By way of punishment. Believe not so.
They would all bear you offerings from good-will:
Due courtesy, attentions from their doors
And hearts, and sympathies the social hour
To animate. But you are proud, and pride
They fear in majesty, aloof themselves
To hold it with a coldness to admire.
To them would you a due complaisance show,
You would find wondrous change, descending then
To be as they—as they to love and be
Beloved. Your grievance would be lost in joy,
And you would live a Trojan Grecian turned.
    An. Ah, how could one indebted so to Troy?
I would dishonor me by such an art,
For nature scarce would give consent. Inhaled
The air of freedom is enthralled; in that
Same freedom I am otherwise than Greek:
This freedom loved, take it takes life in part
Away; what would remain despair would seize
And warp, unworthy reason's oversight.
    Pyr. Your tongue with cold refusal is, the heart
With warm assent! The tongue's words are as winds
Impatient. Lulls the winds the sun, and may
Your bosom words. May you apply that jewel
(Which ever is encased in mortals best),

Whose potency enlightens as a flame,
With thought arising o'er ties intimate,
In universal union with mankind.

　An. Too much is asked. Can woman yield a hold
On destiny? Herself so with it knit,
She feels its strength; is with its knowledge fraught,
Man ignorant—himself a host, unknown
The foe. His feelings less are stumble-blocks;
Her feelings more secure in prophecy.
Thus as she is, you come most politic;
Ask her with self-deceptions, ever prone
To be, turn off from destiny—forego
Her home, her friends, her land—the elements
Of thought that are their fruit—to be half blind
In future! . . . Minerva, the day forbid!.

　Pyr. To be an object of your ire, alas,
Is now misfortune. Wronged you were when fell
Illustrious Troy; *that* terms of war imposed.
It might have been vouchsafed a lot for you
Less rough; *this* made events, not men. In *that*
And *this* absolve you me. As for the present,
Behold you I with kindness doubly deep,
That with it bears the murmurs not full heard,
Its current's depth controlling, better still
For you. Withal, the inspiration yours,
A sentiment my master is, and you
Beholding as a queen see slave, not king.
Oh, woman, know your power upon a seat
Unconscious of a crown! For you it is
To hear, to weigh, to judge, to amplify

Your realm, with king by king petitioner.

An. Ah, so to speak! Your sire remember; he
My Hector sent to seek the shades below.
In widow's plight to stand, forgetting not,
Ought she forgive? My son, too, joy quenched out,
Is sought. As if his mother ling'ring by
It seems—not knowing, lost, as spirit where
To go—as if, approaching, timid, would
Maternal succor plead, his father's ghost
Oblivious of. 'T was dreamed the case was such;
The warm impressions of the memory
Aroused; estranging from what 's now, a pang
Of double motherhood gave birth to more
Than voice can tell. What feelings turn to die
Unworthy are of womanhood; the best
Till end survive, unvariable to do
The service of a life. Then me cast not
Where to belong counts woman void true love;
A graceless figure, not to Beauty known;
A mask-misleading face, her breast half stone.

Pyr. Ah, to yourself still anger speaks. Within
Your bosom nursed, itself it magnifies
By what has been with what fear deems will be.
'T is true, that Troy reduced to formless ashes
A spectacle most melancholy is
Unto the musings of a Trojan's sorrow.
But will they thither go, persist to haunt
Remains of war—grim, crumbled wall by wall,
As tree by tree in winter bare and bowed,
Standing in solitude, awful, speechless?

An. Troy's homes, gay temples, statues, palaces
A medley is of things material—
But ruins for faint shapes!—the raven and
The owl's abode! The winds the heart's abode,
Outlasting iron walls, enduring ever.
The tenants of Troy's dwellings, where are they?

Pyr. Alas, they victims are of circumstance!
Now's solaces invite to other thoughts.

An. How like a Greek you speak!—that quality
Enclosing quality! Ulysses was
As you, attaining by degrees of craft
A final aim of war, to call it peace
In Ithaca! What Trojans dread conferred,
Not on them thrust, is Grecian peace—a gift,
That covets what it gives in claiming due
From foes of rights, of lives the sacrifice.

Pyr. This fact remember kings mere subjects are
As men, that are behind their title, fain
To cast their errors to account of title,
So little they esteem the worth of it.
As kings, they folly do that censure in
The governed moves, who little probity
In them as men allow; whereas, as men
They would kings rectify were but to right,
Law, wisdom, charity the governed true.
Degrees of virtue are a labyrinth
Led through thick briery evils to the haunt
Of excellence. To rule, is ill to one
Committed; doing wrong discreetly is
All rulers' right; and to gainsay this right

(Wherein they would, if could, shine forth as men
Uncrowned) injustice is to kings. Be thus,
Andromache!—desert you not the man;
The king revile, who unto Troy was false
In feeling as Ulysses was in deed—
The king, the people's medium blundering,
Too oft undone, abortive on his throne!

An.   Let this repeated be again, again:
Her fealty is to the absent. Men,
Assuming friendship, seek to break that bond;
And you, as enemy, for this approach.
Avaunt! avaunt!... Why hesitate?... You, king!—
The king of Epirus, the conqueror!—
The author of such evils they obscure,
As clouds, the azure of your glory. When
The north-winds come the zephyrs sigh and crouch.
Thus feelings fresh and innocent withdraw
In dread when come surprising rigors yours,
The dread the more because concealèd they,
From a demeanor's courteousness to burst! ...
Oh, what a land is this, chaotic with
Environments so counter to one's rest!
To find repose, let meditations dwell,
In desert silence, native to the past!

Exit ANDROMACHE.

Pyr.   She goes. Her kind was never seen before.
Her character occasions doubts in those
Who read with common nature life's strange book;
These doubts embarrass so a penalty

They are to bear. Alas, to think makes bold
Obedient to their weight intelligence;
Still not to think deprives; forgetfulness
It is of her and self united not.
It cannot be! A course pursued in fear
An end attractive has; it courage gives,
And heart-rewarding is. Vexations keep
A charm receding just before to whet
The pleasure for attainment soon. Till then,
Let patience be a staff to lean upon;
It can await the hour subjected thus,
Ignoring what amiss to seekers happen.

SCENE II.

ANDROMACHE *and* KALANTHA.

An. Ah, Kalantha, another load of grief
I have to bear to thee. Thy ears are now
With ill news surfeited, despite the times
Which thee would greet to-day with festival.

Kal. Alas, hast seen thy husband's manes stalk
Within the lunar glimpses of green woods?
Thou art so secret with thy steps; so strange
In manner, wild and tame by turns; so prone
To hover by each busy highway at the morn,
Likewise the solitude of ruins chilled by eve.
It seems a fev'rish presence in the blood
Is partly answerable for these thy doings,
Evoking pity from thy wond'ring friends.

An. What stone is this to cast at me? Do they
All pity me? I am, despising it,
Half pity-proof. Plague on a friendship thus!
I would have it exemplify, and bear
A stern approval, watching silently
My vagaries. Were friends, a score or more,
Of mine as I, their trials would prevail
Not o'er the tongue to utter what the heart
Aye hold should, lockèd as in treasury.

Kal. They do not talk of thee; their eyes bestow
Such glances as say more than words; they sigh,
Next turn their faces to the wall.

An.   Ah, well!
Nature to follow thus 't is just. 'T is hard
From what experienced is within to turn;
Still I it all in shame would there disguise,
Leaving suspicion not least espionage
To stand upon. This qualm is pride's—so false!
It would delude itself; deluded be
A glory-bearer of some worth, from it
Estranged because of hollowness. As said,
I would not have these friends me note aggrieved;
And yet, how kind in them to speak of naught
I do or say, but keep it patiently!

Kal. They by sheer means sheer friendship show,
        as well
As gentle instinct that with breeding fits.

An. From me, who Trojan am, Epirian they,
Some gratitude is due. Howe'er I am
Not of their clime: the body here, afar

The spirit, roving in oblivion's dusk,
With memory, a gleam, to pierce this dusk,
Researching for the idols lost. . . . O Nemesis!
What has been done, that to crime capital
Belongs, dispensing by degrees to one
Its opposite, guiltless deeming self?

Kal. Ah, turn to ponder on the days that are!
Within themselves an inspiration is,
As in corn-foliage, Ceres' culture.

An. Yet doubt is here, faith far. Perception has
Too nice a love for joy to seek it where
Treads duty not. This duty is no yoke:
I call it freedom wailing for the dead—
A solace thrilling with heroic heat—
And when one comes to chill this mood all is
Discomforted. Not then the value of
A proffered sympathy I see, so blind
Compassion grows. Ingratitude, a wasp,
Next leaves a wound, that swells, confusing more
And more, until I fain do go betime
To ramble in the melancholy night. . . .
An evil genius one—Pyrrhus—the cause!

Kal. Hath he, pursuing thee, praised civilly?

An. Aye!—more!—he would himself insinuate
Within these arms of love. He bayed is held.
Withal, I fear his eye, it hath such power.

Kal. Oh, do not care for it! He would appease,
Perhaps, thy troubles (too, his own remorse),
In giving thee restored due rights. Regrets
He consequences that averts not war.

An. Mistrusting Greeks, ado is the effect;
And this effect makes errors theirs seem gross.
They are at variance with direction free
And frank: so subtle, fitful, coy and bold,
Is kept the spirit busy to trace aught,
Which traced, is hid at last in secrecy.
'T is hard, confronted thus, to merge with .those
In friendship who, adroit, would alter it
To serve themselves. As for their king, he is
The figure-head of worst and best in them;
So mixed with traits contrary to ideas
Of regal excellence; he crawls or flies—
And in his flight, we think of one just crawled—
And on the ground, of one unfit to fly.
When he is seen to come, I dread to move;
Sensations rising so averse to him,
His shadow on the floor they see, a twin
To one within him darker still.

   Kal. Thou shouldst be woman-like, adapting self
To fair conditions. Brooding, social not,
Thy vision colors what is seen with hues
Unseen by other eyes. To one depressed,
The Orient's splendor laced with silver dawn
Is but a leaden object to the sight. *
What crown is this to thrust aloof? Is this,
Its profferer, unworthy so it seems
Not gold, but brass? When sweet advantage comes,
Oh, mock it not, but nurse it with fresh smiles!

   An. Unknown by thee, why do me violence thus?
Secure from worldly fancies, virtue's sphere,

Life's wingèd element, exalts the mien
From this persuasion thine would have me do.
　　Kal. Soften dejection into genial looks.
It to oppose is friendship's duty. 'T is
An enemy, enfeebling by too fine
A course of sentiment, courageous not.
　　An. Thou art, it seems, his advocate. A meed
In view, thou dost attempt to form a plea.
It, insincere, accords with what expects
A judge, who listens with an ear that holds
A conscience moved by human nature's best,
By it, as by a lamp, the worst well read.
So evident, O woman! servile, guard
Thyself, lest rash turned aloof thou mayst be,
Forbidden a return to my protection.
　　Kal. I would not passive be, nor go too far;
Involved in thought's false mist the medium true
My danger is—and thine! Astray thou, can
I lead thee to the goal assuaging those
Who suffer if due means are me denied?
　　An. Myself shall leader be. Above thy aid
I feel; persuasive aid it is!—to some
Near point, now cherished by thyself, which she,
Thy mistress, must contribute such a share
As will her render servant to obey.
Once more I thee admonish to beware!

Exit ANDROMACHE.

　　Kal. Ye gods! how hard to understand she is!
Deep, deep would intuition peer, her soul

Bare to behold. Why is it I, adept,
Abiding with her long, discern not how
To move her counsels, cherished, hidden, kept
In mystery? With strength uncommon, half
Unsexed, she stands with man's reserve, anon
To pine as woman mutable, and shrinks
As if in superstitious depths to tread. . . .
But let he go! Awaiting, days may come,
Propitious as the breeze to ships shore-bound,
My fortune's drift to favor with their swell.
Meanwhile, prevailing not o'er her (for now
The Parcæ thwart the better to endow),
I 'll to the king, and answer how things failed
In such a way as, still provoking hope,
May lead him farther to espouse more done.
Such game, within the net, well fed will thrive
To feed and fatten who the meat provide.

SCENE III.

PYRRHUS *alone.*

Pyr. With night just gone, not tranquil is the flow
Of after-musings. Sudden changes came
Upon each dream—now fair, now dark. Oh, would
Depart the spell! It as Aquilo chills,
Sending from peaks of snow clouds cumbersome,
With phantoms fraught. Methought, arising from
The bed, my soul, delivered to eterne,

Sojourned within the boundary of the dead.
The atmosphere translucent magnified
Each object far. Sounds echoed e'er remote,
Attuned, serene, divine. All distance was
Contiguity, the centre self, the scenes
In radius unfolding, interfused
With nature-giving arts, nature mystic seeming.
Thoughts vivified arose, existence fresh
(Expressed to them by some arcanum there)
Glad paths to show, ideal and multiform.
Ere long unpurged, unworthy feelings stole
Within, as if controlled by agency
Supreme, remorse to raise, as from the ken
Faded Elysium. . . . Advanced a Shadow soon
To hover and to menace wantonly,
Going, returning oft. Tartarus then
Behold! The Stream of Lamentation slow
(Approaching it, not moving I) rolled on,
Moaning as if a river-god. *Beware!*
Beware! appeared its utterance, as came
A figure greeting, haggard, dolorous,
In glamour's glim to stand. Kalantha she!
I saw, as spirits see—interior—
The fold in fold, that wisdom let ignore,
As dusky Morpheus closed the drowsy dream. . . .
The potency of Heaven at work would baffle
That to this woman holds the key occult!
Alas! too much has been to her confided—
Too much, too much! that should be matter dark,
Known to another not. Offset forthwith

Must be what 's done with what to do—to meet
This woman once propitious, tragic now,
Driving repose e'en from this temple crowned.

Enter KALANTHA.

What have you to report?
   Kal.   Andromache
Opposed was to the tenor of the speech,
That worked with all its skill in your behalf.
I wish to have instructions more forthwith.
   Pyr. How 's she averse—comported she herself
Against the rules of reason, prone to show
The inner workings of an enmity?
   Kal. She censured you so freely, futile was
The tide of her affections to confront,
That do as sea-shells murmur to themselves
A requiem. With eyes that weep she dwells
On Troy. But such things must have days anew
For consequence; these days' fresh thought may give,
Emerging she from widowhood distressed,
A cheerful brow. Time serves congenial gifts
To those that mourn to woo them to forget.
Meanwhile, occasion to assist, I 'll move
Her so (despite her mien, inscrutable
At times), whilst seeming to pursue, as her
Shall lead unto the presence of yourself,
Her eyes then dry, her mood with favors full.
   Pyr. Speaks she of Achilles—of him, my sire,
'Who hardy Hector slew by Trojan walls?—
Of his same corse dragged round the city thrice,

Ere Priam begged his bones dishonored thus?

Kal. Nay, nay!—upon her son Astyanax
Disconsolate she meditates the more,
Though Hector's name is in her mouth. Her heart
Is wounded from the blow that took from her
The babe in such a way as to conceive,
E'en as an image, makes a shudder come;
How cogent more reality!
But this with careful surgery of love,
That cuts to save, that suffers using skill
More than the patient, shall I remedy.
Her memory must of itself have less—
Be dead in part—a portion lopped away—
The past a blank so far as entertains
That which you would not hear. Her leave to me
In this, a woman moulding woman's will,
And doubly able to sustain the effort
In that I hold a phial whose contents,
Once tasted, veers to those who give the mind
Of those who take, subjecting them to go,
To stay, to smile, to cry, to utter aught—
Such is this charm's unfailing efficacy.

Pyr.   [*Aside.*
What artfulness is this! I truly dreamed.

                              [*To Kalantha.*
How came you to possess this you speak of?
It may a drug be baleful; caution must
Foreknow the worst in best. 'T is policy
Before proceeding in an enterprise
To search the dangers out, whilst seeing them

Less fearing them. Be candid then, nor fear.

Kal. Among the slaves from Troy is one adept
In sciences from whom was begged the phial.

Pyr. His name? His habits give, describing him.

Kal. His name, Orgilus. Wrinkled, pale his face
At intervals within the portico
He falters. Once at time of sacrifice,
Bareheaded in the sun, he was seen stand,
As if in act to imitate a priest
In giving oracles; they failed to come;
Next passers-by him taunted, saying: *What
A post is Orgilus!* Another day,
A little skeptical, we turned an ear
To him, his converse to invite; ere long,
Addressing him with kindness, he with thanks
Each favored all. In time him innocent,
Not deep, we found. He reads the stars; the earth
Is nature at his feet o'er-flowered ever.
Guileless, discourses he of Cadmus oft;
Of Saturn's advent and the age of gold.
The gods revering, he would evil thwart
And virtue aid; hence we confide in him.

Pyr. Hath he acquaintance with Andromache?

Kal. He her observes from far, nor dares to step
Across to her. Reserved in modesty,
He would not come e'en if invited once.

Pyr. Your friendship warm, 't is plain, prevails
O'er him, else he would not commit to you
The philter. But, in this, *your* need, not hers,
Not mine, may have procured the means to bless

Yourself; if so, your zeal 's excusable.
Still should it prove its means before to use
In this one case, wherein success comes not
Save through the medium of alacrity,
So hard to move in Andromache bowed. . . .
Where did you see this modest chemist first?

Kal. Within far Troy surrounded by the Greeks.
The bondmaids heard him tell of Helen oft;
Of Sparta and the heroes of that land;
Of Menelaus, the husband wronged, in ire.
In dialect uncouth he spoke, and held
Famed Troy would fall this Helen unrestored
To the besiegers; next, the city sacked,
Would Trojan slaves be scattered in strange lands.
He lives with us to see his words fulfilled.

Pyr. Do know aught else of him? Associate
Does he with men that meet in crowds? What trade
Hath he whereby to eke his master's profit?

Kal. Scarce more I know of him, this more is that
He is reputed versed in prodigies,
For having roved from land to land—to edge
Of seas surrounding all the earth—and divers
Races mingled with, he such tales can tell
As multiply our fears of foreign parts
And make us love our home. . . . He knows no men
As friends, 't is said; he labors 'gainst the wind,
That puffs him back, where intercourse invites
The gossips hereabout. . . . His trade unknown,
Involved in privacy, conjectures he
Arouses, lodging all alone. He seems

His master, yet is not. He fortunes tells
Betimes, receiving humbly coin therefor,
Yet is as proud as Phœbus of his breed.
Modest, still bold, or vain or real, it is
His merit chief he hinders false insight,
Living in peace, a tortoise to the world.
  Pyr. Enough discovered. Here your guerdon take.
Go, woman, to your dwelling. Unto those
Who may what 's passed between us turn to know
Be statue-dumb, inquiry to frustrate.

Exit KALANTHA.

Ah, yes!—go, handmaid, teaching not amiss,
Though evil. Thus embroiled unworthily,
Compunction showeth justice hath in me
Concealed itself to rise, with warnings where
To go. Thus government celestial moves
In darkness, otherwise to lead than where
Allure would foolishness, and makes us sage
Through tests severe of operations slow.
Henceforth my life within is life without,
Exchanging phantasies for verities,
Along decades to move to age, controlled
By what it seeks in best of nature all.

Enter ORGILUS.

What, man, intruding here! why so?
  Org.   O king!
The step intrusive comes, but held in leash.
My wife here entrance found, 't is said; and fear

With busy visions breaks propriety,
Into your chambers searching. She a drug
Of deadly agency purloined hath from
My closet, it believing love-inspiring.
I would from her possession rescue it,
Lest fatal consequences follow suddenly.
   Pyr. Your name?
   Org.   Orgilus mine. Kalantha hers.
   Pyr. To Andromache go—quick!—find her there.

Exit ORGILUS.

What adder is this woman! . . . Thus the dream
Proves monitor to higher consciousness!
To a sweet end let satisfaction wed!

SCENE IV.

ANDROMACHE *and* KALANTHA.

   Kal. Disguise thy spirit in the mien that is
Congenial to the lover's attitude
Toward the smile that flatters him. Hide cause,
Effect then tolerate. Were loyalty
Not mine, I would induce myself 't is well
That thou shouldst be in rue, and go from worse
To worse, in hope to see thee in a state
Where envy meanly brings superiors down.
   An. So skillful thou, persuasion thine has voice
Seeming not human nature's counterfeit.
Somehow, candid to be, thou art much feared.

Kal. Oh, say not so! 'T is luckless fortune thine
That utters. Hence, forgiveness sweeten thought
(That welcome might resentment, to thee false),
And fill my mind with musings charitable!

An. Yes, yes! the drug thou gavest me was said
A cordial to be for nerves unsteady—
Those sluices to the brain, exhausted source
Of tears! Thy husband came announcing it
A medicine dangerous. Charity,
Indeed! Dost thou forgive, excusing proffer
This thine with ever ready casuistry?

Kal. It was my husband's carelessness, alas!

An. Ah, says no more! If tainted thou with guilt,
The Furies thee will scourge. But innocent
Let thee the present call. It easy is
To pardon, since for pardon yearn I now;
It seems that I committed have a thing
Impious. Ringing in my ears it comes,
It goes, 't is known not what. Why so for me
Apparent is black Tartarus reserved?

Kal.   [*Aside.*
How she to humbleness constrains my speech,
Assuming what it should, not what it would!
                  [*To Andromache.*
Thou surely art addicting these thy days
To much on earth suggesting Tartarus.
Remember as thou ailest that relief
Extends a freedom clothed in royal robes.
Oh, turn to it! The past is Tartarus.

An. Ah, me! 't is true. It goadeth to the quick

E'en to admit it so. But who of all—
What presence from infernal regions stole
To make on earth this Tartarus, with flame
And smoke, and din of chariots, and troops
Of archers rushing to the fore, and swords
Of slaughter rich in Trojan blood to foam,
And I to breathe a victim here, the siege
Not o'er it seems? Whose figure is it comes
Athwart my meditative paths, and haunts,
And haunts, until thought reckons it a dread—
A hydra moving in obscurity—
A curse in instant time, so sealed in grief
It fade will never in chilled memory?
These answer to thyself, and feel results.

Kal. Pray, cease! Love has its season as a flower;
The autumn frost it kills, then summer's ray
Revives it on the stem: so 't is with love—
'T is nipped; misfortune's chilly north-winds blow;
Then zephyrs come, its fervor to inspire
Again. Thus Nature nature forms with cold,
Then heat; with night, then day; contrasting change
With change in endless course. Then why should we
Allow the half not wished proportioned more
To be than destiny designs, until
Growing it cramps the other half desired?

An. Woman, 't is vain to parley with thee ever.
The all in all walks on thy sandals, earth
To earth, for aye the wingèd element
Prohibited. . . . Hereafter go thy way,
I mine. Thy seed, ill sown, proves false to trust!

SCENE V.

PYRRHUS *alone.*

Pyr. Alas, to be the object of disdain!
No regal rights saved self from its effects;
It lived subdued in glances, made the mien
Its citadel, and darted words to wound,
As slingers cast sharp stones, e'en unrebuked
To do, its liberty in moral power.
Yet I, new-dowered with fresh strength, survive—
Survive the flood. Repulsed awhile the shore;
But stood at last a being stern to breathe,
A slave no more to Neptune's furious scowl! . . .
Remembrance turns and dwells on scenes gone by.
Oh, how, returning from the siege of Troy,
Applauses swelled! Wain after wain of spoils
Enriching Epirus! The slaves in herds
Affected were, and gladly, by that day,
Aforetime woes forgetting. How prevailed
Andromache, with speechless majesty—
With much within herself that ruled men's eyes,
E'en with her shadow, though a captive mourning!
Self learned, though high, from her, though low in
        state,
The space that was between us two; it strove
With what is best in thought, with special speech
A cause in love to advocate, and won
At last—impressing onward with slow art;—
Won, too, the kingdom of fair Epirus!

THE DAUGHTERS OF ŒDIPUS.

THE PERSONS.

ANTIGONE, }
ISMENE,   } *daughters of Œdipus.*
CREON, *king of Thebes.*
NEARCHUS, *a confidant to Creon.*
OFFICER *and attendants.*

SCENE I.—Thebes.

ANTIGONE *and* ISMENE.

An. Unhappy moments! Music heard is none,
Yet ears would hear, with soothing rapture stirred,
This antidote for grief. I would, O life!
Have music for thy sake; on heaven gazing,
Would have thee breathe its primal innocence,
A being better, fresh with beauty's power. . . .
It seems our race, outsprung from Œdipus,
Is doomed to evil, shame and tyranny,
And silent bitterness so prolonged.
Hence I, as from imprisonment, would flee
From self—my race—in expiation not
For that my father did displeasing Jove,
And all earth's watchful, ghostly hosts of virtue.
But no—it cannot be. Here must remain,
Housed up in what I am, my fate my thoughts,
Deep in vexatious I of harsh events.

Is. Thou sayest truly, sister. What we are
We cannot be from it; what us has come

Appears avenging, proper not for those
That love the virtues. Still it is some fault
Lurks in the blood, I often say, that calls
For our chastisement, seeming harsh, yet that
May prove, when this dark fault is cast away,
The function of salvation. Some event
Of happiness, superior far to things
Long suffered, may transpire. Content thee then
In deeming that the worst has passed; behold,
As from a ruin near, arise the walls
Of safety to confound our enemies.

   An. Didst hear the latest tidings that they bear?
A brother's sister thou, and still so cold!
Here, too, thou movest with assurance such
As fancy kindles, counsel prone to give,
Whilst he, thy brother, stark in death, remains
Unburied on the stony, star-lit plain,
The rites of funeral prohibited.

   Is. Believe I hardly it. So fair, so brave,
O Polynices gone! Our brother dear,
Eteocles, interment had. He was
Lamented by his comrades dutiful,
By me not less, affectionate to yield,
My ties of blood out-grieving them, impelled
By friendship and sad ceremony.

   An. Oh, boast not thou!—unbecoming to the hour
It is. Whilst Polynices' body lies
To vultures ready to devour a prey
(To them delivered by his uncle's oath,
Creon's, our guardian, who sits on the throne

Our father graced), be serious with thy will,
O sister! to oppose his will who rules,
Forgetting justice in severity.

 Is. What can I do? What canst thou do? Mistrust
Gives pause to thought to wonder what to do,
And answer leaves us none save that to fear
Our uncle more. Confronts he sympathy,
As thou dost know, with speech of violence,
Making meek women tremble as he strides.

 An. O sister cease! Thy instincts are amiss.
Always understand duty courage teaches;
It would my brother timely burial give.
He otherwise must wander desolate
About the earth, his soul permitted not
To go with Charon o'er the guarded stream
Unto Elysium.

 Is.   Wouldst thou defy
Thy uncle, and, perhaps, the powers above   ,
Himself, that move him oft to do what he
As man would leave undone? Beware, O sister!
It seems thou standest near a precipice,
Half-blind, bewildered, going but few steps
To fall. In falling so, accursèd as
Our brother, thy own body would entombed
Be not. What double portion then for grief!
Ah, me! to mourn thy fate, his fate, to deem
Ye wander vainly both about the earth!

 An. Sister, he is my brother; thine also:
To bury him my duty; thine also.
United thus, our union strengthen we,

For mercy's sake, to find a sepultre
For him forthwith ere Time delay condemns.
   Is. What I thee aid? The king would forfeit ask;
Compel to look on Death, the enemy,
The urn we prize not holding me entombed!
   An. The king!—comes he by what authority
Upon the pathway of a purpose dear
It to defeat? Why fear him so? The will
Of woman, zealous though in weakness, touched
By kindness, makes men turn about in shame,
Dreading the ministry of love's reproof.
   Is. Still let the deed of burial lie within
Ourselves, inaction's child: the gods will know
It there, rewarding what we would with what
We should encountered by impediment.
Is in a passiveness the better course;
It pleases; not in an advancement rash,
Which galls authority, it making lose
Its reason in emotions prone to evil.
Reflecting on we have endured, and this
Endurance ours so long, why ask we not:
*Where is respite, by any source, with balm
Assuaging for awhile?* Come, sister, come,
Let's seek it far—another country in,
Dividing seas a precious space between
Old woes, new joys. . . . Infernal powers, attest
Nowise abet I what is bid undone,
And do persuade against unlawful things!
   An. Alas, go then! Antigone alone
Her brother's body, wetting it with tears,

Shall crown with pious sepulture. Secure
To go, he 'll journey to the Fields, to her
Indebted for the happiness. What more
Demands the conscience for reward than this:
Affection moved through peril right to do;
Affection found fulfillment's anadem?

Is. It is not love of flesh debars to aid;
Though over-hanging shade of danger comes
To startle vision, flesh cares less for it;
This would it undergo, earth's ills permit;
But that so poignant, creeping, essential
Without proportions, evermore enthralling,
I dread. . . . O sister! rouse from reveries;
See death related to thy soul in such
A form that fate to come is pardonless.

An. Unworthy thou, reluctant thou, O sister!
From honor's sacred emblem gone and lost,
In gloom to wander so, and fain to go!
Thy uncle's nature half in rule, thy own
To welcome it too ready with the word!
Ah, well, the funereal rites must mine alone! . . .
Subserve, ye hands, my brother's destiny,
No kindred else a tenderness to add!

Is. If must, then shalt thou *do*—alone! But in
Thy doing keep it private from report:
This much to Ismene a duty is;
Otherwise such may happen dark to name.

An. Expedient one! what time the thunder comes
Thou art abashed; when lightning comes, forlorn.
A bud would face a storm, and thou wouldst shrink!

Is. Thou art, distracted, not conditioned well
To answer what impresses best. Therefore
Overlookèd is contempt expressed by thee.
Another time let passion cool to ashes,
Leaving thy reason to resolve fair things;
Foul things expressive of one's poise are not.
Therefore, sorrow awaiting, joy will then
Receive one true as sister dear restored.
Oh, may the hour be soon! Till then, adieu!

Exit ISMENE.

An. Ah, well, Ismene goes! Her absence means
Much to Antigone. Appears it she,
Now gone, hence better seen, is not the person
Thought pictured to myself: of womanhood
The proof lies in the deed, not in the guessing.
How frigid her demeanor! Heart, how hard!
Of pity destitute, dry to the taste
Of noble feeling doing noble work,
And deeming those thus actuated lost
Within the feeble mazes of distress! . . .
From this, O sister! turn I now; to thee,
Dear brother, go my steps. It seems impels
Thy ghost. May action favored be! If so,
Thy bones inhumed shall be; thy soul appeased
Shall from its dismal state descend
To Charon's boat, embarking to attain
Elysian Fields, thy kindred to rejoin.

7 - G

SCENE II.—In Creon's palace.

CREON *and* NEARCHUS.

Cre. What rumor this that stirs? 'T is said, the law
Defied, that Polynices' body hath obtained
Interment. Who the traitor that would do
This thing? He 's free, unpunished for a time;
More fatal be the hour detecting him!
If what is said be true, confirm it so.

Ne. No further know I than from rumor comes.

Cre. Why bid you trace the rumor to its lair?
Unconscious else to what the crown is due.
Still falter not to go to find wherewith
To case from doubt.

Exit NEARCHUS.

These Argives bold, of whom
Was Polynices chief, may have through zeal
Their courage left approach too near the mark
Forbidden, cast defiance at law's means,
By which they would, upraising, steal within
The sacred limits of imperial rights,
An by usurping be authority
Unto authority, subjecting by some chance
The very kingdom to plebeian feet. . . .
How vexed to note ambition's seething sea;
To meet cajolers ever to the front;
To know that shadow near, hypocrisy;
To hear, e'en by the throne, those stingèd whispers
That hint at hand of fell conspiracy,

To breathe in struggle soon, opposing hate
To hate, and shield to shield, in bloody bounds
To execute! A mark for obloquy,
In these sore tempest-times, his silence art
To veil those self-endearments that make kings
Mere men, and that make fears, and these those acts
That men, not kings, despotic call, the lot
Of Creon is! Hence, how with tact impartial,
Yet ones unruly holding in a course,
To act, evades at times the will; is blurred
The judgment, breeding for humanity
Distrust, for self likewise. Thence thought refers
To Heaven for light in darkness—torch to guide
The steps—to move the atmosphere of minds,
With favors fraught, obedient they to view
Their best in him, their king, sustaining one
Another with accord. But Heaven is dumb.
Hence, he must still the mask of hardness wear.
The people know the face, the heart unknown.
Then face be king, implacable as night
Concealing soothing day, the heart of time! . . .
Appears it Thebes, despoiling now herself,
Sits weeping by a willow near a stream
(As yet veiled, robed as mourning widowhood),
As if in knowledge of careers ordained
Her children, grim and soon, to overhaul
With irony. Events control events,
Having no cause in that of mankind worthy;
They tend not from a something worst of past
To a something best, future's purgative.

Till then, the goddess Peace will not to Thebes,
Bearing aloof what would rebel. . . . Discord,
O Œdipus! was from thyself. Thy sons
Their father proved in simulating thee;
Now all the base results from what thou wast
Encounter hour by hour a censure futile:
It powerless; surviving, they o'erwhelm
As waves o'erwhelm the eddy of the shore.

Enter NEARCHUS.

Ne. It is too true!—delivered to the tomb
Hath Polynices been. The people stare
And marvel at the deed, dispersing as
In fear when questioned as to him so bold,
So law-renouncing, so confronting risk
As thus to tread the field of legal danger
In doing it. Appear, sheep-eyed, they as
Those who tend to forbidden paths were once
The wolf away, their leader now not seen,
Mysterious. What notes suspicion near,
Much more imagination notes afar,
Mingling what is within with that without,
Until my breast enkindles doubt on doubt.
     Cre. What, what!—hath Polynices been interred?
Curse it!—What traitor hath interment given?
Curse him!—Who do concealment help in this?
Curse them! . . . Ye witnesses above, ye gods,
Remand the guilty ones to justice sudden! . . .
When happened the event?

Ne.   A time most e'er
Conducive to the men of treason, worst
Then doing—in the ambush of the night.
  Cre. Thus danger comes and takes us in the back;
It uses darkness still unrighteously.
  Ne. Alas, too true, with overreaching stealth!
  Cre. 'T is well to hesitate in quest; lest he,
The doer of this wrong, should bear the palm
Of victory in feeling that distrust
His work beholds, and flee the consequence.
  Ne. Let vigilance, not words, investigate.
  Cre. Let scruples seek an art too fine for men,
Appropriate to kings, men to undo,
Who with their bluntness act, betraying them
Little by little to the judgment seat.
  Ne. Let silence then be bait to trust.
  Cre.   Treason
To find is task for instinct; still to lose
For reason to amend a failure hard;
For this, be silent altogether not,
As words are arms stragetic when well used.
  Ne. Let silence be to words a monitor.
  Cre. What man or men can be suspect in this?
  Ne. Of this one here, of that one there 't is known
Enough to follow to their haunts, at last
Them to detect in some offense that would
Debar their liberty; but these confound,
Not clear decision guilty ones pursuing.
  Cre. Then do what 's well, arousing senses all,
In such a way as will take note of much,

Your mask indifference, until the game
Comes in the range of a conviction sure.
Till then be shrewd; be officer to none,
But citizen to all; in converse move
Congenial to the common flow of talk;
Meet smile with smile, regardless of the proof
Borne in the face of things of mischief done.
Thus acting, have for model nature near,
With movements none unconscious of a part
That one, not acting, would to failure sink.
Thus trained, depart, all Thebes a hunting field.

    Ne. Nearchus goes. Let duty be the soul,
Accomplishment the body of intent;
The latter awkward moveth to an end,
The former would unerring what it should.
Then blame not him if all is not success
Subserving you, for aught amiss may hap.

Exit NEARCHUS.

    Cre. Yes, yes! Nearchus goes, the sycophant!
So eager to observe observing vain,
He makes forms familiar strange, and forms
Uncommon usual—thus he crawls, though man! . . .
O royalty! why not abandon thee?
With all I am, with purple clothed, makes that
To alter not in self to relish what
Grants plain simplicity a hermit knows.
To bear compunction; this awakes a touch
Of wild desire self would not have; yet it

Maintained abides. Believing that accused,
Of daring eyes the stigma, disappear
The purer feelings once familiar!
Not fear, bosom's Eumenide, relents;
No virtue it expels; no succor comes
Persuading it to go afar. . . . Then Sleep,
O Sleep! as ancient as the earth on which
We dwell, so powerful to bear thy balm,
Approach from shrouded mystery with dreams,
Effacing what is felt with deep repose.

SCENE III.—An area by the palace.

ANTIGONE, ISMENE, NEARCHUS *and* OFFICERS.

Is. O sister dear! the king doth know the deed;
A spy hath traced it to thy door. Thou art
Condemned by many, others grieving. Still,
Thou must with self-denial soon do more—
Thou must avow what 's done.
An.   I live in this:
I would not seek the favors of the world
Departing from myself, to leave behind
Within a better comfort than is found
Without. So colored with profanities,
So counter to philosophy this world,
I know not how to bend to him, the king,
Its head, its heart, without upon myself
Inflicting sorrow. Still I 'll go to him,
Confession make, yet free within to shield
A potency, and feel in silence blessed.

Is. With thee shall go I then, conjoint to say
Was Ismene a prop to this, thy deed,
By him detested, ready to endure
What comes expressive of his vengeance certain.
 An. Oh, do not have it so! Thou didst oppose
What was the prompting of my heart with what
Was from thy mind. 'T is not becoming thee
To offer now to stand, with such a mind,
Thy sister by the sentence to receive
That her is due in fullness of effect,
Because the cause was hers.
 Is.   Reprove not so.
My duty owed to thee its wisdom choice;
Pretending, it meanwhile supported thee
With that from thee concealed. Now comes it forth.
In sympathy it feels for thee with such
A warmth that this thy cause is mine, whereby,
Beginning thus anew, in union now
We are, assuming equal amnesty.
 An. Sister, thou dost delude thyself. How couldst
Thou have been with me in thy soul, when thou,
With tongue so ready, didst upon my heart
Cast wounds that only partial rancor gives?
Surely, an evil phantom at thy ear
Made thee indifferent to thy brother stricken
Whilst so involved in anger's hastiness
Me to frustrate in his behalf.
 Is.   Alas,
I did but try to waken to the risk
Most oft encircling those infringing laws.

The risk thou didst not fear. Thy eye dwelt not
On outward things; thy mind, content with what
It held, supplied the sight with sacred rites
Proceeding from thy tenderness. Absorbèd so,
It natural was to study to alarm
That preservative sense that bids us all
Take care of self. Revolving o'er thy lot
To come, departed from thee I as shook
Each limb impatient. Know my love for him,
Our brother, is as thine; withal for thee
It is as strong; then why should I have quit
This love for thee to leave thee deviate
In not availing of all that is mine
Of reason and its ministers to draw
Thee from thy peril? Sister, see aright:
How stood my motive that was puzzled much
What course to follow to advantage bring
Unto our common selves, whilst came the hope
That he, the king, relenting, might permit
The funeral pile unto our brother dead.
  An. Why dost thou to such means resort as balk
An understanding of thy womanhood?
Thy variance is oft masculine, oft deep
In method, semblance hiding much, I am
Half loath to call thee sister. Why to me
Be not a twin in fundamental love,
In mental concourse one, obscuring naught
Thus bound? Apprising thee so prone, my words
Are on my lips ere time takes time to form
Them into syllables, and ere I know

What 's said 't is said. I can not hold account
Of what I feel or think or do from thee devoid
Of those sensations which rebuke with such
A force regret is mine. But thou art swayed
With such conditions 't is a mystery
To solve that we are kindred of one bed,
Save by an instinct faintly knowing each
As brute knows brute.

  Is.   Sister, no more!
Thou art unjust in judging traits of mine.
I know not how it is; but confidence
Withheld is modesty discreet, or tone
Of manhood curbing woman's mouth, or ill
Within the blood of candid words afraid.
As thou, I am in dark about the matter.

  An. Is felt what thou dost say is so: a cloud
Doth settle o'er me, keeping indistinct
Much that I, curious, would perceive. Although
Too close in speech, reserved to give where well
Thy secrets not, yet blameless thou. Still there 's
Within thee, counterpoising to my wish,
Some quality that on occasions thoughts
Evoke, admiring faintly, drooping soon;
At others, selfish censure that this wish
Would have thee hear for penalty: in this
I go below myself, in that above; in both,
A medium false, discerning I not clearly.
Oh, could we mortals eke our day's scant light,
What virtues would adorn its sentiments!

  Is. Pause, sister, pause! Without this area gaze.

Who 's yonder coming scanning all around?
Nearchus! Seems his shadow him before
Advances, dragging him behind. As wont,
He mutters 'tween his teeth. He sees us not.
Let us retire within the peristyle.

An. Ah, no! I would not have myself confess
Thus so a cowardice to consciousness,
That would, despite the faults it bears, sustain
Not this. Let us confront him with a look
Of honor, aid to innocence, if so
We can. . . . He turns to us. I would not fear,
Yet fearing thrills. He is the king's own spy,
Tigerish. Comes he! Sister, lend thy arm
To bend, supporting me, around the waist.
He nears! Let 's turn away; my breath is short.

Is. No, no! let us retain our ground. Now hap
What will, we must the worst with strength repel,
Forsaking not the best some end to gain.
The gods behold, with whom resides our weal,
Dividing it for those here disappointed.

Enter NEARCHUS.

Ne. Ye trembling aspens, what a scene presenting!
Ah, well! . . . The king, Antigone, in wrath
Hath spoken, intercessors vain. Many
From him in apprehension turn. Accuse
Thee others, saying thou at night hast sinned
In giving forms of burial to the one,
Who˙traitor to his country, was outlawed.

Now, what misfortune thine! What grief for it!
The king, in terms repeated, hoarse, declares
Aversion for the heirs of Œdipus,
Anathemas succeeding as he hears
The late injunction violated is.
Oh, say thou guiltless art, and thus relieve
Suspense that hangs mist-like about all Thebes!

   An. The deed was mine. A sister's right impelled
To wish a brother's bones immunity
To have from fowls devouring flesh therefrom;
His spirit gifted, loved so well by many,
To enter Pluto's bounds, arrested not
By Styx, the Fields Elysian to extend
To it their welcome. Well reflected I
On what was due to him, on what was due
To Creon; weighing these confused, was chosen
The firmness of my love for leadership,
That held obedient every faculty
Of grosser nature to accomplish this
You censure so. The consequence was known,
And knowledge half prepared my fortitude
To aim at no evasion power provokes—
To die if need be. Having for reward
The joy of doing well, joy 's conqueror.

   Ne. To such would further listen not my ears.
Would eyes behold thee friendly to the state,
Its pillar clothing as an ivy thou!

   Is. I, too, am guilty, scorning the impulse
That lurks within, suggesting phrases veiled,
That would aught hide, insidious to avert

The blame; the ostracism; the penalty
Most stern imposed by judgment's seat. To her
A relative I am; together we
As children played; we are as women bound
By ties so mutual they most precious are
Unto ourselves. I knew beforehand what
Was her intent, inclined to yield as is
Her wont to mercy's call. I sympathized
With her in part; yet failed I her to hinder
In the accomplishment. Ismene thus
Is guilty, wishing thus to stand with her.
   Ne. Thou, too, false subject to authority!
   Is. Yes, let our uncle, Creon, hear it so.
   Ne. Ah, well! I, messenger, to give to him
Who circumspect implored, forbidding me
Awhile with accusation none to join! . . .
Having well-wishes in respect to you,
His nieces, he especial for your sake
Won praise from those, your opponents, who were
Most quick to cast suspicion on your backs.
Then still he favored you when rumor came
More pointedly arraigning you, with proof
So positive it made him tremble—cheeks
Both pale, eyes both uneasy. Came anon,
Assailing him, his wish to hear them not,
Such words, such phrases and such sentences
Concerning you as chafing him he burst
With passion, full persuaded that the truth
Alone you charged exactly. Thus from him
I came, and found you here, O guilty pair!

An. Return to him and say Antigone
Will yield to the outcome, yet with assent
Seeing no law. At first she wept to think
Creon's decree to break; but having it
Once broken, so enforced with faith that what
She did is right, above the awe of kings,
With better purpose proud she stands. . . . Alone
I am in this, and she, my sister here,
Is innocent; return and tell him so.

Ne. Antigone, have pity! Bid me take
That thou as she art innocent, a task
Much lighter! Trifling is the falsehood.
Thy guilt, a heavy load, must cause remorse
More grief than falsehood aiming for thy weal.
A life's own fortune lies within thy mouth;
A whisper is enough. Dost understand?
Then utter it, oblivious not of friends
Who wait in doubt and anxious for thy safety.

An. No, no! in fear of gods, my thoughts not less.

Ne. Still pity me, for go I unto one
Who, inexorable, is rash to act,
Compassion crushing, fiery in revenge,
His end attaining by the surest course!

Exit NEARCHUS.

Is. Alack, alack! Impressions come that make
So dizzy now the brain things are amiss.
Aught inimical now influence would,
Turning virtue's motive out of doors! . . .

Recede let us to some near place retired;
There let us sit, assuaging senses all.
Something may yet be done us from to loose
The fatal tangle making to involve
Our lives, to perish by degrees. . . . Oh, thou
Hast been bewildered from thy better self
By a false deity, hell-born, profane,
Thy frailty to mislead, apart to act
Against prerogatives of innocence!
    An. Be not afflicted. Thy true self, away
From thee, will come again. Remember, fear
Is at the heart where courage was before;
Thou didst inspire me with it now not more
Than half an hour. I feel its tone as yet
Dilating as harp-sounds the drooping head.
Oh, what half phantoms we as women are!
We are embodied in too false a mould,
That, not all ours, or fickle, rash or wise
Makes us, the sum oft small, the kind oft poor.
    Is. Oh, this is not a time for utterance!
I want to be alone. Oh, go awhile
Away! A heavy sickness by the heart
Thy presence aggravates, disdaining thoughts
Of duty that would fortify the will,
In sympathy with thee, to be more strong.
    An. I go. . . . Resolve, my master be. I turn
From tribulations of life's day to calm
Of death's near night. . . . O flesh, dim servitor!
Thy mission done, sink in oblivion's flood;
Thou art of earth—mere dust. . . . O soul, adored!

Be now my all, supreme; with speed direct
Me from where flesh is now to where 't is well,
Salvation there, its presence serving, bowed
Before the humble. . . . Nerves, be strong! I would
Not quaver now in what intent conceives,
Lest shame might conscience burn, and form
On it a scar forevermore. . . . Thus, thus!—
Fare thee well, sister, fairest Ismene!—
Whilst dauntless is the mood I must be going.

Exit ANTIGONE.

Is. What can she mean? The figures of her speech
Abstruse! But that her custom is, impulse,
Doth bear her forth. A heart of dove, a wing
Of eagle, too, both hers! Still in her features
There something was unusual e'en for her.
My words may have offended her; if so,
Herself restored to love will come again
And smile on me. . . . This head doth ache and ache.
What drowsy numbness this that lulls my tongue?
'T is well she 's hence, repose a panacea.

Enter NEARCHUS *and* OFFICERS.

Ne. Ismene, what appearance this! Upon
Thy cheek a snow-white pallor is. This day's
Sad business, unsettling to strong men,
Hath called for austere bearing of ourselves;
But thou, one delicate, succumbing now,

With firmness gone, art proof, indeed, of what
The struggle costs. Condolence bends to thee;
It would not, futile, tender what it hath
To aid distress. Withal, it would not go
Too far; it hath intelligence it shrinks
To tell. The torrent of the times brings down
Disasters on proud heads. Impious thought,
Though suff'ring moves to it, dares not reproach
The gods, for evils are their plagues men due.
Let patience be the gospel then of mortals—
Mortals that blend as mist in ether high
With immortality, Time's province fairest!
This good should be the chief to instigate
Our progress through the moments trying us. . . .
Thy sister, Ismene, hath more than erred;
Her trespass Creon rouses more and more—
A lion rampant he. These officers
Standing hard by he sent with mandate clothed
According to his wish. Dost know the rest? . . .
Thy sister, where is she?
   Is.   I do not know.
Just ere you came she left. She here will be
Anon. She 's much disturbed, and wanders to
And fro. Her hair disheveled fell adown
The back; her garments loose the zephyrs seized
As if in wantonness. Two passers-by
Did look on her with sorrow joined to awe,
Shaking their heads as they moved off. I should
Have gone with her. He mien bewildered so,

8 - II

A chain it is that to itself may link
(So heavy now with weight accrued!) more harm.
But here I am, and she aloof. She here,
There I should be. She should be Ismene,
And I Antigone; for grievance drugs
Me so the worst I would have happen me,
Not her.

    Ne.   Which way went she?

    Is.   I think without
The city's walls toward yon cypress grove.

    Ne. Officers, thither go; if her you find,
A prisoner of state with her return.

Exeunt OFFICERS.

    Is. How cruel is the king! Yet you are kind;
For you would hide what he determined has.

    Ne. In self-esteem find courage to assist.

    Is. To know the terms precise he has imposed
The ear just now to listen would recoil.

    Ne. Still know, prophetic shadows hover near.

    Is. As fears the bud the frost, so hope fears them,
Chilling the ardor of warm maidenhood.

    Ne. Take time awhile assuaging fear aroused.

    Is. What 's best, that would, were mercy's news
Vouchsafed, be bright, dispelling vapors thick
Which rise, enshrouding from occurrences;
That would awhile, surmising, fain believe
That all is well, and what is present past,
Making the future golden, promising.

Yet 't is foolishness!—jargon!—vagary!
Stands Reality before with mantle dire,
Material as the flesh in which breath is,
We facing where, ere long there, perish all. . . .
Nearchus, then say on! Be foul or fair
The tidings, speak of Antigone's fate.

Ne. The king gives forth she shall alive be cast
Entombed, atoning for her late offense.

Is. Oh, loathsome sentence, from an uncle, too!
To die shut up with perturbations strange!
The mould, the worms each vital moment seizing!

Ne. I would friend's comfort give; my functions bid
A cold performance of command. . . . Behold,
An officer approaching here in haste.
What can this signify?

Enter OFFICER.

What, ho, man! Where
Is she for whom you have been sent? Foot-speeding,
Such tells of some mishap betiding late.

Offi. She—Antigone—the others guard her form.

Ne. Ho, ho! give voice, and stammer not, its words.

Offi. Within the cypress grove, at mouth of cave,
Her body lies, stabbed to the heart. Blood red
Flows on the lily whiteness of her breast.

Ne. Some one has murder done!

Offi. In dexter hand
She clasped the dagger jealous of her life,
And self-infliction helped it to its work.

Ne.   Art certain, man, it is Antigone?

Offi.   Certain! Upon the temple's marble steps,
Ascending she to worship, have I seen
Her frequently, as people nodding said:
There goes Antigone, soon Œdipus,
Her father blind, to lead.   How filial she!
Then on she moved amid a general hush.
Unlike she was to any woman else
In Thebes, so dear to high and low! Now sleeps
That figure (swine it snuffing when we saw
It first) ne'er to awake again.

Ne.   Let 's hence.
This work will anger more the king.   Thus foiled
His mandate, breed it may annoying hints,
Until his palace with contention sounds.
But go to her at once, then go to him.
Come, come! delay answers effect not well.

       Exeunt NEARCHUS *and* OFFICER.

Is.   Now, think of it!—so warm of late, now cold!
Her virtues turned to a sad monument!
Oh, would it were not so! . . . Desert me not,
O strength! I would have thee support these limbs
E'en to the green spot where she lies.   But how
Is this?   Frailty with crippled gait is here
Instead, when I should hasten to her corse—
Ah, there should go all out of breath, and cast
Me down, and weep affliction out.   She gone,
My father gone, my brothers gone, and I

Alone—these things possession have. A numb
Sensation steals, as poppy's dreamy fume,
Arousing then depressing efforts made,
That waning would resign. This knot on knot
In woof of present to unweave repels
Less skill than Fate's; but she in distance grim,
For race of Œdipus admonishment,
Is as a thunder-cloud. Then joy is sin
When Time atonement for fatality
Invokes, to answer stage by stage unto
The tomb. . . . Antigone, all spectral now,
Thou art so severed from this earth, the loss
Not its, but Ismene's—so much, no gain
From other one existing can restore.
Removing to a bourn, in that reserved
In shadow-land no footstep to invite
Pursuit behind, I would be old more near
To be the path on which, descending now,
Thou art at peace; I would be old, forgot
Youth's weariness, to feel soft tremors come;
The fading day of self into its night
To undulate. . . . But how is this? Oh! Oh!
How sight doth fail! The footsteps halt! I would
Recline somewhere. Not here. Where shall I go?
Each sense, how dull! . . . O Antigone, me return!

> [*She swoons.*

THE END.